A Terrible Roar

of WATER

A Terrible Roar

of WATER

Penny Draper

COTEAU
BOOKS
FOR KIDS

This novel is a work of fiction. Names, characters, places, and incidents either are the product of the author's imagination or are used fictitiously. Any resemblance to actual persons, living or dead, is coincidental.

Edited by Laura Peetoom
Cover photo by Candace Cochrane
Cover painting by Aries Cheung
Cover and book design by Duncan Campbell
Printed and bound in Canada by Transcontinental Printing
The inside pages of this book are printed on recycled paper, 100% post-consumer fibers.

Library and Archives Canada Cataloguing in Publication

Draper, Penny, 1957–

    A terrible roar of water / Penny Draper.

(Disaster strikes ; 5)
ISBN 978-1-55050-414-9

    I. Title. II. Series: Draper, Penny, 1957- . Disaster strikes ; 5.

PS8607.R36T46 2009   jC813'.6   C2009-903500-6

10 9 8 7 6 5 4 3 2 1

COTEAU
BOOKS

2517 Victoria Avenue
Regina, Saskatchewan
Canada   S4P 0T2
www.coteaubooks.com

Available in Canada from:
Publishers Group Canada
9050 Shaughnessy Street
Vancouver, British Columbia
Canada   V6P 6E5

The publisher gratefully acknowledges the financial support of its publishing program by: the Saskatchewan Arts Board, the Canada Council for the Arts, the Government of Canada through the Book Publishing Industry Development Program (BPIDP), Association for the Export of Canadian Books and the City of Regina Arts Commission.

To Ila
For inspiring me with your
love of Canadian history

CONTENTS

PROLOGUE 1

CHAPTER 1: NOVEMBER 1929 5

CHAPTER 2: CUT-THROAT 13

CHAPTER 3: THE KITCHEN PARTY 26

CHAPTER 4: WHEN WISHING STILL HELPED 43

CHAPTER 5: BELLA 52

CHAPTER 6: A TERRIBLE ROAR 59

CHAPTER 7: RUN! 75

CHAPTER 8: A LITTLE SHAKE 83

CHAPTER 9: GOOD NEWS AND BAD 87

CHAPTER 10: ANNIE 97

CHAPTER 11: MURPHY'S LIST 109

CHAPTER 12: THE S.S. *Meigle* 123

CHAPTER 13: RORY'S PLANS 134

CHAPTER 14: ARE MUMMERS ALLOWED IN? 139

AUTHOR'S NOTE 149

PROLOGUE
The Burin Peninsula, Newfoundland
May 1917

THERE WAS A FIERCE CRY. BELLA, EXHAUSTED, *opened her eyes. Nurse Cherry was triumphant.*

"It's a boy!" she smiled, thrusting the swaddled bundle into Bella's arms. "You have a fine baby boy, my dear. Do you have a name?"

Bella smiled down at the baby. He made little grunting noises as if surprised at his new world. "My husband Noah knew we'd have a boy," said Bella happily. "We're going to name him Murphy. It means 'sea warrior'; did you know that, Nurse Cherry?"

"I did not," said Nurse Cherry. "A strong name, to be sure."

"Yes, Noah is sure our boy will love the sea, just as he does. 'We will fish together,' Noah said, 'my boy and I.' Noah will be so happy, Nurse Cherry!"

All of a sudden, there was another fierce cry from out in the kitchen. A few moments later Bella's sister Rosie appeared at the door of the bedroom, her husband Randall filling the doorway behind her. "Bella, oh, Bella!" Rosie wept. Rosie ran to the bed and clutched both Bella and the baby. "I'm so sorry!"

Bella was bewildered. She looked up to Randall in confusion.

"Bella, it's…there's been an accident. A terrible accident. Noah…he got caught in the line. It twisted…well, his foot…he got pulled overboard. We couldn't get him back."

This didn't make sense to Bella. What did Randall mean 'they couldn't get him back'? Lots of men fell overboard from fishing boats. They got pulled out. The fishing went on. She shook her head. "Where's Noah?" she asked.

Randall looked to his wife for help. Rosie was still crying. He sighed. "He's gone, Bella. Your husband, your Noah, he's drowned. I'm awful sorry."

The room went very still. It was Nurse Cherry who spoke first. "Well, then," she said. "Well. A mother and a widow all in one day. This is a terrible trial to be sure, but look to the good, young Bella. Look to your fine, healthy son." Nurse Cherry was known throughout the Newfoundland outports to be a practical lady.

Bella, white with shock, looked down at her tiny son. He would not fish with his father. All those pictures she had imagined in her mind's eye — they were all gone. Noah lifting a chortling baby Murphy high over his head with glee; Noah teaching a young Murphy how to jig for capelin; Noah and a grown Murphy working side by side in their fishing dory. All gone. Who would teach her son to be a fisherman, to be a warrior, to be strong?

All these thoughts ran through Bella's mind. But the words she spoke came from a different place entirely.

"We will starve," she whispered.

CHAPTER 1
November 1929

MURPHY BIT HIS LIP. HE SQUINTED HIS left eye. He could see the small shadow circling below him; he could feel it. Murphy prepared. One shoulder up, a small twist to the right. Stick out the tongue and hold it just so. Two jerks up, let the hook sink, another twist, and –

"Gotcha!"

Murphy flicked the fish onto Uncle Randall's stage. The motion made his unruly mop of brown hair escape from his knitted cap. Murphy impatiently jammed the cap further down on his forehead as he regarded the growing pile of good-sized capelin. Murphy was pleased. Uncle Randall's stage was the best place in the outport to fish for capelin. The stage was a wooden dock that stretched a good distance out into the harbour. At the water end was a large shed where the whole family gathered to process the fish when the fishermen came home with loaded boats. Murphy felt ready to go out on one of those boats. He was strong and nimble, even if he did look a little scrawny. After all, he could always catch more fish than any of the other kids. Murphy had a knack. Aunt Rosie said it was in his blood.

But it was time to quit for the day. Murphy glanced over to where the other kids were jigging for fish. Sean and Fiona, his younger cousins, were doing more playing about than fishing, as usual. His buddy Martin had a good pile. Even Annie, the little kid next door, had done pretty well for a girl. She was eleven, a year younger than Murphy and very annoying, but she could fish.

"Well, if it isn't the Capelin King. Trying to out-fish me?" came a sarcastic voice.

It was his cousin Rory. Murphy whirled around and looked way up. Rory was tall. "Of course not, Rory. You're a real fisherman. You catch cod. Capelin's nothing more than baitfish. I know that."

"A r-e-a-l fisherman, wow. Kid, get this: there's nothing impressive about being a r-e-a-l fisherman. Take my word for it. Stick to the land."

Murphy was puzzled. "Why are you so mad, Rory? Did something bad happen out in the dory today?"

Rory looked at Murphy. "It was no worse than any other day, kid. They're all bad." Rory stashed his fishing gear at the far end of the stage. "Why you even want to go out there is beyond me!"

Rory strode off towards home. Murphy stared after him. He just didn't understand his cousin. How could anybody *not* want to be a fisherman?

Rory was his oldest cousin, ten years older than Murphy. He was already a man and had Uncle Randall's dark looks and fierce blue eyes. Murphy was next oldest in the family. Aunt Rosie had lost a couple of babies after Rory. That's why she'd been so eager to take Murphy in after his dad got drowned. After Murphy came Fiona. She was eight and the only one of the family who had inherited Aunt Rosie's red hair. Fiona had the temper to match. Last came Sean, who was just seven and still a baby as far as Murphy was concerned. Aunt Rosie said that Murphy was good luck because she hadn't lost any more babies after he came to live with them. Murphy had his doubts about the luck thing. He was born the day his dad died – how lucky was that?

Murphy dumped his capelin onto the splitting table in the shed. Taking one of the sharp knives from the wall, he quickly gutted the fish and cut off their heads. He washed them clean in salt water and loaded them into a bucket to take home. Aunt Rosie would be waiting for them.

Hollering to Fiona and Sean to get a move on, Murphy walked to the end of the stage and set his feet on dry land. Aunt Rosie's house was just a stone's throw from the water's edge, as were all the houses in the outport, each close to their own family stages. After all, every family was a fishing family and a stage was where the work got done. It was handy to have everything built so close. Seventeen families lived in their outport, with more families in other villages up and down the coast of the Burin Peninsula in Newfoundland. Mostly there were no roads, but footpaths connected some outports across the rocky headlands. Others were only accessible by boat. That was all right by Murphy. He didn't need to go anywhere, unless it was out to sea.

"Thanks, Murphy," said Aunt Rosie, when he gave her the bucket of fish. "It's a good lot. Get the kids washed up for supper, will ya? And I'll need some more wood brought in." Aunt Rosie was round and warm and jolly. She liked to pretend she was fierce but she really wasn't.

Supper was fish and cabbage. Again. Fiona complained. Again. She hated cabbage. Murphy figured she better get used to it, cause he was pretty sure they'd be eating it forever. Never had there been a year like it for growing cabbage. Pickled or boiled, they had it every meal. Aunt Rosie had barrels of pickled cabbage in the cold store, and shelves of head cabbage stacked up on shelves ready to freeze when the weather got cold enough. At least there was molasses bread for afters. Murphy brought in water for the washing up and as

Aunt Rosie and Fiona tackled the dishes, he debated about taking a look at his homework. Nah. Surely there was something better to do. Uncle Randall saved the day.

"Murphy, the weather's looking good for the morning. It's late in the season, but we may just get one more day's fishing in. It's been a right fine season. Rory and I'll take the dory. Be ready at the stage when we come back, will ya?"

"Uncle Randall, can't I come with you? I mean, I got to learn the sea sometime, don't I? I'm old enough and I'm real strong. Please?"

Uncle Randall exchanged a quick glance with Aunt Rosie. He looked back at his nephew. Murphy was small for his age and, like all the outport people, he was a little thin because of his diet of fish and vegetables. But Murphy was strong. Even his hair was strong; his brown curls were like springs. They constantly escaped from the knitted toque he wore every day. He had warm brown eyes; his face was brown too, from being outside all the time. It was a quiet face, but an honest one.

"No need rushing into things, lad. Tell you what – you can be my cut-throat tomorrow. You've a careful hand with the knife, I've noticed."

Murphy sighed. It was better than nothing. *Little* kids just got to bring water and fetch salt and kick the fish guts down the hole in the stage floor. At least he wasn't one of them any more.

"That reminds me, Murphy, you got a letter from your mom today. It's on your bed," said Aunt Rosie.

Murphy brightened. He liked getting letters from his mom. He only got to see her once a year when she came by schooner to visit him for his birthday. Her letters made up for the in-between times. They were always long and newsy, full of words. He guessed that made sense, since her job in the city was all about words. She was a telegraph operator in St. John's. All kinds of messages and news came through her telegraph. Some of the news was real interesting, and she would tell Murphy about it in her letters. She told other people too. His mom told him that so many people asked her about the news that she started writing it down in a book. Folks would come to the telegraph office and read all about it. Some of the folks couldn't read and asked her to read the news out loud to them. When his mom told him that, she asked him how his own reading was coming along. "It's important to be able to read, if you want to get ahead," she told him. "Make sure you keep at your lessons. Maybe you can come to St. John's to go to school one day."

Ha! That was never going to happen. You couldn't fish from the city.

Murphy didn't exactly know why a fisherman needed to know how to read. They needed to know the tides and the habits of the codfish and how to mend a net and the right amount of salt to cure the catch. But he, Murphy, was different. He needed to be able to read his mom's letters. And he liked being the first kid in the outport to know stuff. So he paid attention to his reading lessons, even if he cared about nothing else in school.

Murphy flopped on his bed and opened his letter.

Dear Son,

I have lots of news today. My telegraph has been going quite mad. It seems that rich folks down in the Boston States and other places like New York City are having money worries. Look up New York in the atlas, dear, so you'll know where I'm talking about. The people there trade in money instead of fish and all of a sudden their money isn't worth very much. Folks who used to be rich are poor, folks who used to have jobs don't, and there's a lot of upset about that. You can imagine. I'm glad you live in the outport. If the fish aren't worth much in trade, at least you can still eat them!

Murphy rolled over on his back. He'd never been much interested in money. Like his mom said, it wasn't very important in the outport. They traded fish for whatever they needed at the store, stuff they couldn't grow like flour and sugar and tea. It worked out. Uncle Randall had some paper money hidden in the Bible. It was only paper – how could it be worth anything anyway?

Murphy smiled. His mom always had interesting stuff to tell him. He knew it was kind of strange not to live in the same house, but it was better that way. The two of them couldn't have survived in the outport without a man to fish for them. That's why he wanted to get out on the fishing dory. When he started to earn a share of the family catch, he could bring his mom home.

Anyway, you'll probably hear about it on the radio. The newspapers are calling it 'Black Tuesday.' No worries for you, though. Aunt Rosie tells me it's been a good year for fish and a great year for cabbage. I bet Fiona's complaining!

That's all for now. Be a good boy, do your chores and mind your aunt and uncle.

All my Love, Mother

Murphy put the letter down and stared at the water stain on the ceiling over his bed. Boy, he missed his mom. He wanted her home for good. Why did it take so darn long to become a fisherman?

CHAPTER 2
Cut-Throat

IT WAS STILL DARK AND VERY, VERY COLD. Murphy knew that Uncle Randall had said no, but it didn't hurt a body to try, did it? He pulled on the long underwear that Aunt Rosie had knit for him, a pair of black pants, his jersey, his sweater and his oil-skins. He pocketed two pairs of mitts and his toque. He even remembered his handkerchief, jamming it up his sleeve as he grabbed some hard bread from the kitchen shelf.

Aunt Rosie handed him a bowl of brewis with a wry smile. "The men'll say no, young Murphy. Mark my words. You'd be better off in bed, letting your bones grow to man-size. Don't be in such a hurry!"

Murphy dipped the hard bread into the hot salt-cod broth. As the bread softened, he reached for some scrunchins to sprinkle on top. He loved the crunch of the fried pork bits. Jamming a huge bite into his mouth, he shook his head.

"Gotta go, Aunt Rosie," he said, spraying crumbs all over the table as he did.

"Murphy!" spluttered his aunt, cleaning up the mess. "Maybe he is a man," she muttered to herself. "Sure eats like one!"

Murphy walked hopefully down to the stage. It was the last trip of the season. Surely they'd let him give it a try? But as he got close, Murphy could hear Rory and Uncle Randall arguing. Both men looked up at the same moment and saw him standing on the stage. They stopped talking. "Murphy, throw me that line," called Uncle Randall. His face looked craggier and bleaker than usual. He and Rory both jumped into the dory. "Push us off, there's a good lad." Murphy knew this wasn't a good time to ask. He watched them row away from the stage and join other shadowy boats heading for the end of the harbour.

"Drat!" Murphy felt like stamping his foot. "They'll never let me grow up!" He turned on his heel and stomped back to the house. Aunt Rosie was kneading the bread dough and she gave him a small I-told-you-so kind of smile as he went by. Murphy threw off his outdoor clothes and climbed back into bed.

A few hours later when the sun was actually up, Murphy opened his eyes for the second time that day and stretched. Over his second bowl of brewis, Aunt Rosie laid out the day.

"Men'll be back with the first lot by noon. Murphy, before that we need the hay brought in to the back shed. Your uncle's got it raked and nicely dried in the meadow. The weather's holding just fine but you can't be too careful. I've already milked the cow and fed the pig. Fiona, skim the cream and pour it into the churn; you need to make some more butter. And watch the bread. It's in the stove but I'm too busy to watch. Let it burn and there's no dinner for you today! Sean, I've saved the pot liquor from the brewis for old Mr. Chester. He's feeling poorly. Take it down to him, will ya? Then go down to the stage and start getting ready. Haul a couple of buckets of water and make sure there's enough salt."

Aunt Rosie stopped to take a breath. As she did, Annie from next door came into the kitchen and headed for the daybed. She shrugged off her gumboots, curled her feet under her, tugged the hem of her faded plaid dress down over her bony knees, then stuck the end of her long red braid in her mouth and sucked it.

"You look comfortable, sittin' there like somebody's pet pig," smiled Aunt Rosie. "Trying to escape chores, are we, Annie?"

Annie's green eyes twinkled. When she grinned her freckles danced. "I wish. Coming here *is* my chore. My mom wants me to give you a holler," she said, twirling the braid around her finger. "My little sister's got the earache. She's right bad, Rosie; can ya help? Nurse Cherry's gone up the coast."

Aunt Rosie sighed. "Course, dear, I'll be right there." She looked at the pot of melting animal fat on the stove. "The soap can wait." Aunt Rosie always made soap in the fall after a pig had been slaughtered. There was lots of extra fat on the pig, and she'd boil it down, then add canned lye and boil some more, until it was a soupy mess. Then she let it harden so it could be cut into neat bars of soap. Her soap was much prized because it smelled good. Everybody always asked her how she put the nice smell in, but she never told.

Aunt Rosie moved the pot off the heat. "Come on now, Annie, I'll show you how to make her feel better. Ya got an onion?"

Having delegated the day's tasks, Aunt Rosie bustled off next door. Murphy fixed an eagle eye on his young cousins. "You heard what your mom said, right? So get on it. I'll be out in the back."

Hay for the winter was important, but as the family only had one cow and one horse the amount needed was manageable. Murphy reckoned he could finish and still have time left over before the boats were back. Maybe he'd go down The Gut and see his buddy Martin. Murphy worked like a demon and the sun was not yet overhead when he was done. After checking on Sean and Fiona, Murphy headed along the footpath to The Gut.

The Gut was a narrow neck of water at the far end of the harbour. Martin's house was built practically on top of the water. It was a prime spot. Good spots were handed down from father to son, so there wasn't much opportunity to move about. This worried Murphy. His own father's spot was long since taken. Was there any place for him?

Just then, Murphy heard footfalls behind him. He turned, and there was Annie.

"What are you doing? Are you following me?" he demanded. "Aren't you supposed to be looking after your sister?"

"Mom and Rosie are. We sliced an onion and put it on her ear. My chores are done. So I'm going with you."

"Are not," retorted Murphy. "Martin and I got things to do."

"I'll do them with you," said Annie blithely.

"Will not. It's not girl stuff."

"So what kind of stuff is it?"

"Not for you kind of stuff."

"So, really," said Annie thoughtfully, "you don't have anything to do and you just don't want me around."

"Yeah, that's pretty much it," agreed Murphy.

"Too bad!" laughed Annie, as she skipped ahead on the path. "Martin! Martin! Where are you? Murphy and I are here!"

Murphy groaned. Girls.

Martin wasn't finished his chores, but his mom let him go, seeing as he'd have to be back soon to help at the stage anyway. The three of them headed up the scrubby hill that rose from behind the houses. From there, they could look down the length of the harbour right out to the Atlantic Ocean. Like mussels in a tide-pool, the houses formed a ring around the edge of the harbour. The stages looked like wooden tentacles stretching out into the water. All the houses were pretty much the same, except for colour. Made of wood, two stories high, stage in front, garden in back, long clothesline across the garden with clothes always blowing in the wind. Each roof was sloped but not too much, otherwise the wicked northwest wind that blew would take that roof and blow it out to sea. There wasn't a tree in sight that was higher than Murphy's waist because the wind wouldn't allow such a thing. There was something clean and fresh about all that wind.

"So," said Martin. "Where you going to put your stage, Murph?"

"You're getting your own stage?" breathed Annie. Murphy sighed. *That's* why he didn't want her along. Too many questions.

"Well, I got to, don't I?" said Murphy. "I can share with my uncle for a while, but if I'm going to support my mom I've gotta do better than that. Thing is, I need a good spot."

Martin peered out over the harbour. "How about there?" He pointed.

"Nope. Swells are too big there. The dory would bounce around like a rubber ball anytime I wanted to unload my catch."

"How about over there?" Martin pointed again.

"Golly, Martin, remember what happened over there last summer?" spluttered Murphy.

Martin looked blank. Murphy looked meaningfully at Annie. "Remember when we rowed that old dory over there to check out the spot?"

Still Martin looked confused. "No, did we really?"

Murphy shook his head in frustration. "And we…ah…ran into a little trouble?"

"What kind of trouble?" Murphy shook his head at his friend's memory. Annie was hanging on to every word.

"Trouble with a…hard object?" How many hints did he have to give?

Martin's face lit up. "Now, I remember! That's when we put that huge hole in the dory when we ran into that rock!"

Annie shrieked. "That was you guys? Boy, were the men ever mad! How come you didn't own up?"

"Why do you think?" grumbled Murphy. "Are you going to tell? Jeepers, Martin! How could you?"

"Of course not," said Annie primly. "I'm not that kind of girl. How about there?" She pointed to a spot on the headland. It was right at the mouth of the harbour, largely unprotected from the sea. Murphy squinted.

"The wind would blow the house right into the water," he said.

"Not if you built it higher up. See, there." Annie pointed. "There's a kind of ledge in the headland. Tuck the house in there. The ledge would give it some protection. And between the house and the rock there'd be lots of room to build a cold storeroom for winter vegetables. The back garden would be higher up the slope. A bit tricky maybe but the vegetables would get lots of sun. Just build a ramp for the wheelbarrow along that slope there. See?" She pointed again.

Murphy had to admit there were possibilities. He was thoughtful. "No," he finally decided. "It wouldn't work. The stage would be right out in open water. The storms would take it out every winter."

"Not if you built the stage sideways," replied Annie. "Instead of sticking it straight out, curve it around the coast. The dory can unload on the lee side close to shore, and the wind would blow alongside the stage, not across it. It would hold. I'm pretty sure, anyway," she added as an afterthought.

"It would be too far from the house," Murphy persisted.

"Is that such a bad thing?" asked Annie. "My dad says we build too close to the shore anyway. Makes for shorter walking, but what if the water rises? What if we get a big storm? Building higher up is different, but maybe smart."

Murphy was flabbergasted. It actually *could* work. "How do you know all that stuff?" he asked Annie suspiciously.

"I listen," she shot back at him. "My mom says the women around here do more than half the work. I guess we have to do most of the thinking too!"

Murphy was saved from any more discussion by the sight of the fishing dories rounding into the harbour. First load was in. The three of them got up and raced for their family stages.

By the time Murphy arrived at the stage, puffing from his run, Aunt Rosie and Fiona had already donned their oilskins and headscarves. Sean was busy hauling water. Murphy got his gear on, laid the knives out on the splitting table, then grabbed the pew. The pew was a long, one-pronged fork that the fishermen used to spear the fish from the boat and heave them up to the stage. As soon as Uncle Randall's dory came close, Sean threw his dad the lines and the boat was made fast. Murphy threw the pew to his uncle as Rory climbed out of the boat. Right away he could tell that Rory and his uncle had been arguing. There was a thickness in the air that made Murphy's innards shrink. What was wrong with Rory these days?

Without missing a beat, Uncle Randall began to pitch the fish. Each one had to be stabbed through the head, not the body. The "pronger" had to be careful if he wanted to keep the value of the fish high. Murphy took first position at the splitting table. He was the cut-throat. It was his job to take a sharp knife and, with a deft movement, cut the throat of each fish, then slice down its belly. He passed the fish to Rory.

Rory was the header. He dug his fingers inside the carcass and found the precious liver. Pulling it out of the fish, he dropped it into a special bucket. The livers would be used later to make cod-liver oil. Then Rory pulled out the guts of the fish and tossed them down the hole in the floor of the stage for the tides to wash them out to sea. Last, he positioned the fish with its head hanging off the splitting table and, with a flick of his knife, lopped its head off. That always made a loud pop. The head fell down the hole and the body slid across the table, right into Aunt Rosie's hands.

Aunt Rosie was the splitter. She made two quick cuts in the fish, slicing down to the tail then back up. Then she removed the backbone. This was the second most important job. If she made the cut wrong, fish meat would be lost and the fish would be damaged. The family would lose money.

Next, Fiona took the split fish and washed it carefully with sea water. Not one bit of the guts could remain, or maggots might breed in the fish and the catch would spoil. As she washed fish at the end of the line, Sean kept the fish moving at the front of the line. It was his job to make sure the hole was kept clean and that all the guts were washed clean away. Cleanliness was everything.

The last job, the salting, was the most important of all. Both Uncle Randall and Aunt Rosie could do it, but Rosie was best. As soon as Uncle Randall had finished pronging the fish, he took Aunt Rosie's place at the splitting table and Aunt Rosie moved to the salting.

At the back of the stage was a series of wooden boxes called fish pounds. Aunt Rosie placed the split, washed fish in careful layers in the boxes. When one layer was complete, she took a handful of salt and sprinkled it over the fish. It looked easy, but Murphy knew better. The salt preserved the fish. Done correctly, the fish would last and fetch a good market price. Done wrong, the fish would rot. Aunt Rosie had to take care to sprinkle only a little salt on the skinny parts of the fish, and more salt on the thick bits. It took skill and experience. Aunt Rosie was an expert.

Time was of the essence. The more time the sun shone on the dead fish, the more likely it was to spoil. The family worked hard, each doing the job she or he knew best. Their lives depended on it.

Cut, split, cut, split. Even through his gloves, Murphy ended up with nicks and cuts every time. A fisherman's hands were nasty to look at – all those cuts, and the fingers got badly crooked up from holding the lines and gripping the fish knives. It was just the way it was.

The family worked quietly at first, concentrating on the job. But once they got the rhythm going, Uncle Randall started to sing. Fishermen knew lots of songs. Aunt Rosie joined in. She couldn't sing at all. Oh, she tried, but she couldn't carry a tune in a basket. That's what Uncle Randall always said. It didn't matter. Singing was like breathing when you were working at the stage. Finally Rory joined in; his voice always made Murphy smile inside because it was so deep and gravelly. Lately it had been harder and harder to get Rory to sing, or do anything with the family. Murphy could tell it made Uncle Randall mad and Aunt Rosie sad.

As soon as the splitting was done, Rory and Uncle Randall got back into the dory to set their nets a second time. Aunt Rosie looked up from her salting for just a minute to watch them go. The two men pulled at the oars in perfect rhythm. She shook her head and sighed. There was perfect rhythm on the outside but not on the inside. Murphy stared after them wistfully. Aunt Rosie smiled at him, then went back to the fish.

Murphy, Fiona and Sean had only just finished sluicing out the stage when Rory and Uncle Randall came back with the next load.

"My, you've done well!" exclaimed Aunt Rosie.

"For late in the season, this is a gift," agreed Uncle Randall. Everyone in the family took their places once more. Cut, split. Cut, split. Their oilskins were covered in fish guts. Their hands leaked blood from all the nicks and cuts. Their gloves were soaking and beginning to stiffen as the sun went down. Still they worked. Toes grew cold inside gumboots. Still they worked. Uncle Randall lit the lamp in the shed. It burned with cod oil and was smoky. The light wasn't very good, especially when the wind blew in from the door and made the lamp swing from side to side, casting crazy shadows everywhere. Even though he was used to it, Murphy's nose began to wrinkle at the smell of dead fish. He was tired.

Sean, who was only seven, had been hauling water for eight hours without one complaint. He knew better. But he was almost asleep on his feet.

"Take the little ones to the house, Murphy," Aunt Rosie commanded. "Get yourselves a bit of salt beef from the barrel and there's some molasses buns in the pantry. Don't worry about heating enough water for a bath, but give'em a bit of a clean, will ya? When they're in bed you can come on back down."

Murphy put down the knife and tried to unclench his fingers. It took a couple of minutes to rub some life back into them.

"Come on," he called to Sean and Fiona. "Supper."

Murphy fed the kids, washed them as best he could and got them into bed. They were both asleep in seconds. It had been a long day for everybody. And it wasn't done yet. Grabbing another molasses bun, Murphy got back into his oilskin and gumboots to help with the cleanup.

Murphy walked out of the house chewing his bun and closed the door behind him. For a moment, he stood there in the dark. Every stage was alive in the dark, with flickering lamps casting an odd light across the harbour. Bursts of song or laughter rang out from one stage or another. The houses, in contrast, were mostly dark, with the very young sleeping safe in their beds.

It was safe; it was beautiful; it was home.

CHAPTER 3
The Kitchen Party

THE NEXT FEW DAYS WERE BUSY, BUSY, BUSY. After the fish had been cured for just the right amount of time in the fish pounds, they had to be taken out and laid to dry on the flakes. The flakes were great wooden racks covered with dried boughs. Even Murphy had to admit that moving the fish was awful work. They were heavy and wet with the moisture the salt had drawn out of them. Each fish had to be washed again and then laid out in just the right way on the flake. The women of the outport were experts in knowing how to spread and pile the fish for perfect drying. It had to be perfect to get a good price from the fish inspector. The other thing the women had to do was watch the weather. The good part was that none of the kids had to go to school, because they were all on call at a moment's notice to cover the fish if a squall blew up. This late in the season, all the fishing families worried about bad weather.

Being on call suited Murphy just fine. He had good ears and good legs, so as long as he listened carefully he could pretty much do what he wanted and still get to Aunt Rosie whenever she called for him. It was a good time of the year for soccer with the guys, or would have been except for Annie.

She just wouldn't leave him alone. Why couldn't she play with Fiona? Sure, Fiona was only eight but they were both girls, weren't they? Why couldn't they go away and do girl stuff and leave the guys alone? But Annie stuck to him like glue. The idea of building a house on the headland for Murphy's mom had grabbed her and she wouldn't let it rest.

Murphy had to admit the idea had captured him too. One afternoon Murphy decided to make his way out to the headland. He didn't need Annie; she wasn't the only one who could think. Maybe he could see if the shoreline really would be okay for a stage.

Murphy headed up, back behind the house to the meadow. That's where the outport animals grazed. He dug up a carrot for Ember, the family horse. Sean was the horseman in the family. He loved the animals. For the rest of the family, Ember was just a workhorse, able to plough the garden and haul the wood, but Sean truly loved him. Ember was okay, thought Murphy, as the horse delicately nibbled the carrot. But a boat was better. Mrs. Moulton's sheep were milling about. They were just beginning to look fluffy as their winter wool grew in. Silly things, really, but Murphy appreciated their wool. Aunt Rosie and the other women spent the winter spinning it and knitting it into jerseys and long underwear for the men.

Behind the meadow was the forest. That's where the men spent most of their winters, inland, cutting firewood and trapping animals to eat. There was a path that ran between the meadow and the forest that headed towards the headland. Murphy walked along it, scheming in his head. To bring his mom home, he'd need a house, a dory, a stage and a flake. My, there was a lot to get done.

When he got to the headland, Murphy had a grand view of the harbour off to his left and the sea off to his right. The spot was a ways off from the other houses, but not so far away it couldn't be managed. The path from the outport was overgrown, but that could be fixed. But so high up! Annie was crazy. It couldn't be smart to build your house on such high ground. Think of all the walking you'd have to do, going back and forth to your stage! You'd have to carve stairs out of the rocks. She was right about the ledge, though. Murphy paced off a house. It would tuck in there quite nicely and that was a fact. And the upper meadow wasn't too boggy. It would make a reasonable garden, as long as the wind didn't blow it to pieces.

Murphy sat down and looked back at the outport. He had to admit the location wasn't bad. But it wasn't good either. It was just too high.

But Annie wouldn't let the idea die. Every time Murphy ran into her she was talking about it. And that happened a lot, since she lived just next door. Finally, in desperation, Murphy agreed to go with her to the headland and show her why it was a bad idea to build there. Annie was so excited her freckles nearly danced right off her face. And she didn't listen to a word he said. Every time he thought of a reason why the location was bad Annie told him how to make it good. She was like a leaky roof. Drip, drip, drip, drip – she never let up. It drove him crazy. So he reckoned the most sensible thing to do was give in. Maybe it *would* work.

After that, the two of them spent all the time they could at the headland, building and planning. Murphy just had to be careful not to let the guys know or they'd laugh right out loud. First, he and Annie dragged driftwood up the rocks to the ledge where the house was going to go. They built a little shelter up there. The driftwood made pretty good walls, but finding a roof was harder. They couldn't find any left-over tin anywhere in the outport. But, like magic, one morning when they got to the headland they found a perfect square of corrugated tin caught in the rocks by the water's edge. It must have been washed there by the tide, although where it came from was a mystery. No matter. They hauled it up to the ledge and tied it down with bits of rope they found. It had an amazing view; even Murphy had to admit it. And hard as it was to climb up the rocks dragging the wood, once the shelter was done it was really cozy on the ledge. Annie started to play house right away, bringing bits of food and even a chipped plate from home, but Murphy wasn't too interested in that sort of thing. He needed a stage.

It was hard to figure out where the dock should go. One afternoon when Uncle Randall was busy Murphy "borrowed" the dory and he and Annie rowed to the headland, tied the boat to a bush near the shore and let the dory drift. Once they figured out exactly where the current was, they poked stakes into the water to mark out where the stage would go. There was just enough room for the stage and the dory. The stage was the first thing to build, Murphy decided. He just wasn't quite sure where he'd get the lumber. But he'd get it.

It turned out not to be as hard as he thought. The very next day Annie came running into Rosie's kitchen to yank him outside. As she pulled him up the hill to the meadow, Murphy anxiously checked to make sure none of the guys were out and about. He wondered, not for the first time, how it was that Annie had talked him into all this. She was just a girl, for heaven's sake! She ran ahead of him, red braid bouncing off her back as she ran. A little ways ahead she stopped and pointed triumphantly to a spot of ground beside the path. When Murphy caught up, worries about what his friends would think left his head. There, just beside the path, was a stack of old lumber, all higgledy-piggledy. It hadn't been there the day before.

It took them all day to drag the lumber to the headland and most of the next to attach the lumber to their stakes. They didn't have any nails, but tangled up in the old lumber had been lengths of old rope. They tied the stage together. It wouldn't last forever but it looked just like the real thing. Murphy felt proud.

One day Murphy found an old net snagged on a rock near his new stage. It had a lot of holes, but it could be mended. What a find! Annie was busy building a table with rocks for their little shelter up on the ledge, and Murphy let her go ahead while he worked on the net. He almost felt like a real fisherman.

The project was going so well that Murphy forgot everything else. It was a shock when Aunt Rosie got up one morning and decided it was time for them all to go back to school. The fish were practically dry. While she bustled about making snacks, Murphy tried to become invisible. He didn't put his school clothes on. Aunt Rosie gave him the evil eyeball but he ignored her. He was twelve; he'd had enough school, thank you. He could read and write, and knew his numbers well enough to keep a tally. He had more important things to do, although he couldn't tell Aunt

Rosie that. Murphy pretended not to notice Aunt Rosie until finally she sighed.

"Enough, Murphy. Get dressed. I made your mom a promise that I'd get you educated best as I can, and I'm keeping that promise. Here's your snack, now go!"

He was stuck. Grumbling, Murphy pulled on clean clothes and grabbed the lassie bun wrapped in a handkerchief. He couldn't even remember where he'd stashed his homework. Nor did he care. Murphy pulled his lips into a thin line as he left the house so Aunt Rosie would know how put out he was without him having to give her backtalk and getting in trouble. She didn't seem to mind his glowering expression, however. She just stood at the door with her hands on her ample hips and watched him go. Drat, drat and double drat. He hated school.

It wasn't even a real school, he grumbled to himself as he walked along the footpath. It was just a bunch of the kids going up to the church. The church was the only building big enough to hold all of them. The priest taught them reading, and sometimes a schoolteacher would stay for a few weeks at a time and teach them arithmetic, with maybe a bit of history or geography. Pretty much all nonsense, thought Murphy. Why did he care where China was?

The day was about to get worse. Most of his buddies were already in the church when Murphy slid into a pew beside them.

"Where you been, Murph?" asked Charlie. "We ain't seen ya around." Murphy tried to figure out how to answer. He sure couldn't say he'd been playing with a girl.

"Just around," replied Murphy vaguely. "Helpin' out and stuff."

"Helpin' Annie, ya mean!" said Martin slyly. Murphy closed his eyes. Why did Martin's memory only kick in at inconvenient times?

Ben whistled with glee. "Pickin' em a little young, ain't ya?" The boys laughed. Luckily, the priest rapped on their pew with his pointer.

"Boys, pay attention!"

But it wasn't over, of course. Annie came right up to Murphy during the morning snack break to talk to him.

"After school let's go to the headland. I've got something important to show you."

Didn't she know anything? Murphy gave her the cold shoulder right away; he had no choice. He could tell she was hurt, but what was a guy to do?

"Not now, Annie. I'm busy. Go away."

"Murphy! I gotta show ya something!"

"Not now, kid!" Murphy pushed past her. Under his breath, he said, "Later, okay?"

"No!" Annie stomped her foot. "There's going to be a kitchen party tonight. We can't go later."

"Well, I can't go now," retorted Murphy rudely. "Go away."

Murphy promised himself he would stay away from Annie for the rest of the day.

AFTER SCHOOL THE GUYS WENT DOWN TO THE harbour. The men were checking the nets and the handlines, sorting through the ones that needed repairing over the winter. Murphy loved listening to the men talk. Aunt Rosie called it "being a fly on the wall." Nobody notices a fly on the wall, so the fly gets to hear everything. Murphy liked being a fly.

"Boy!"

Murphy started. Was somebody actually talking to him? He looked around the group. It was Annie's dad. "When do you think you'll be ready to go out on the boats?"

"Right now," replied Murphy without missing a beat. The men guffawed.

"Hey, Randall, you got a real fisherman here, don't you?" Uncle Randall looked over at Murphy with a bit of a smile. "Enthusiasm, now that he got," said Uncle Randall. "Experience, well, that needs work." The men nodded gravely. Not one of them had forgotten Noah's death, even though twelve years had gone by. Fishing was serious business. And Randall had a great responsibility, raising another man's son to the sea. He was right to be careful.

The men turned their attention back to the nets. Murphy felt that familiar flash of frustration. How was he supposed to get experience when nobody let him do anything?

"Anyway, there's no rush," went on Uncle Randall. "I've got Rory here to help." Murphy looked up at Rory in time to see the flash of anger that crossed his face.

Aunt Rosie cooked supper early. As she ladled out the vegetables, she commanded them all to eat up. "I'm baking a pie to take to the party. No afters until then. Stay out of my way."

Murphy was happy to oblige. He settled down with his scribbler instead.

Dear mom,

Things with me are ok. Uncle Randall won' t let me out in the dory. Pleez tell him Im big enuf. Last catch is on the flakes. Nearly dry. It was a good season. I' m cut-throat now. I really like it. It' s better than gutting. Not so squishy. The bones kind of sound crunchy. Sean' s water boy. I wish yu could come and visit. We' re having a time tonite. I hope Mr. Inkpen comes to tell storys. I' m tryin to think of a good riddle to tell.

Aunt Rosie called for everybody to get cleaned up before the kitchen party. Murphy was able to scratch a few more lines to his mom while he waited his turn.

> I found a place to bild us a house. Ill try to do it as fast as I can so you can com home. Annie found a place and she's helping. I'm still not sure it's a good place. It's way up high and to far from where I bilt my stage. But I'll sort it out. Don't worry, mom.

Maybe he'd finish the letter tomorrow. Then he could tell his mom about the party. It was at the Hillier's house. Murphy could hear the laughter leaking out their kitchen door well before Sean was ready.

"Hurry up, slowpoke!" he said to his cousin. "We'll miss the storytelling!" Sean was trying without success to slick down his cowlick. He'd put so much grease on it Murphy reckoned you could fry an egg on his head if you wanted. He sighed and got a rag to wipe some of the gunk out of Sean's black hair. Murphy made him brush his teeth again because he had cabbage stuck in all the cracks. Poor Sean, his teeth were as crooked as Mr. Chester's fence. Sean struggled with his tiny shirt buttons so Murphy helped, and finally the last one was done up and they were ready.

"Murphy, you carry the pie. Fiona, take the lassie buns. Let's go," called Aunt Rosie.

It was a cold, clear November night. Everybody, young and old, came to the kitchen parties. Murphy took a quick look around and made a mental list of everybody who was there.

Mrs. Moulton and her knitting needles

David and Jessie Hipditch and their three little ones

Old Antoine, a retired sailor from France

The Kelly family

The Brushett family

The two old sisters, Mary Ann and Elizabeth Walsh. They had to be a hundred years old. Each.

Mr. Hollett, the magistrate for the peninsula, and his wife

Mr. Bartlett, who ran the store

But mostly there were Hilliers, lots and lots of Hilliers. Nan and Herbert Hillier and their four kids; the Hillier grandparents, Henry and Lizzie; the Hillier uncles, Tom and Chesley: there were Hilliers everywhere. Inside Mrs. Hillier's kitchen, a group of men were gathered around the Waterloo stove, discussing how much better off they were than the folks in New York who'd lost all their money on Black Tuesday. "I've got fish to trade, barrels of vegetables to eat and tons of coal to keep me warm. I'm better off than those rich fellows!" blustered Mr. Brushett.

"Hear, hear!" replied the other men.

The women were laying out the food on the kitchen table. Some of them had babies in their arms. Murphy looked some more. The Rennies had arrived as well, and that meant Martin was in the crowd somewhere. Yup, there he was with his younger brother Albert, both of them trying to steal lassie buns from the sideboard. Murphy laughed when Mrs. Rennie slapped Martin's hand playfully.

Mr. Rennie called out. "Where's Mr. Flynn? Where's our fiddler?"

"Ack, he'll be along," replied Mr. Hillier. "No need to wait for the instruments. Let's have some chin music!" The children, most of whom were piled up on the daybed, started to clap their hands. Gumboots began to tap out a rhythm on the bare plank floor. A good strong voice started to sing.

> I's the b'y that builds the boat
> And I's the b'y that sails her
> I's the b'y that catches the fish
> And brings them home to Lizer.
>
> Sods and rinds to cover your flake
> Cake and tea for supper
> Codfish in the spring o' the year
> Fried in maggoty butter.
>
> I don't want your maggoty fish
> They're no good for winter
> I could buy as good as that
> Down in Bonavista.
>
> Hip yer partner, Sally Tibbo
> Hip yer partner, Sally Brown
> Fogo, Twillingate, Moreton's Harbour
> All around the circle!

More voices joined in. "I'se the B'y" was a favourite song; everybody knew it. Then old Antoine Miller moved to the centre of the floor and started to dance. Instead of the usual gumboots, Antoine had worn his hard-soled shoes and my, what a noise they made on the wood floor as he step-danced up a storm.

Before long, Mr. Flynn arrived with his fiddle. With him came Mr. Flanagan and his accordion, the one he called his squeezebox. And Jim Best brought his ugly stick. It was the ugliest of all the ugly sticks in the outport! Jim had "borrowed" his wife's broom handle and attached all manner of noisy bits to it. At the top was a big tin can, painted up to look like a face, a really ugly one. An old mop made the hair. A whole lot of tin bottle caps with holes punched in were strung together in loops, nailed up and down the broom handle. Jim had added a couple of tin cans for good measure, making a fine rattle. An old holey sock covered the bottom of the stick. Jim started to pound that ugly stick on the floor the minute he entered the kitchen; at the same time he hit the ugly stick with a smaller stick that he carried in his hand, making the bottle caps rattle to the beat of the song. With a pounding and a clanking the music officially began.

One by one, everybody took a turn doing a jig. When old Antoine was done, Mr. Rennie stepped up, then Annie's dad. Aunt Rosie danced with Sean and

Murphy danced with Fiona. Mrs. Hillier danced with her sister, Jessie Hipditch. Feet were flying, hands were clapping and music rang out through the dark – it was a time.

The kitchen grew warmer and warmer. After a while, the dancing slowed as the people tired. Everybody was waiting for old Mr. Inkpen. He was the best storyteller in the outport. As they waited, Mr. Bartlett, who ran the store, shouted, "I'll tell you a merry riddle to while the time away!" There were cheers all around.

Four legs up and four legs down,
Soft in the middle and hard all around.
What is it?

There was silence. Then a voice sang out "a bed!" There was laughter all around, then an expectant hush. Another voice called out.

What is that which belongs to you
But others use it more than you do?
Another silence.

It was Annie who figured it out. "My name!" she cried. Boy, thought Murphy, she really was smart. Without missing a beat, another riddle was thrown into the air.

Old Mother Twitchett had but one eye,
And a long tail which she let fly,
And every time she went over a gap,
She left a bit of her tail in a trap.

That was tricky. Murphy thought hard. He wanted to get this one. One eye and a long tail. Tail gets caught. In what? Was Mother Twitch an animal in a trap? No, animals have two eyes. Something else. Murphy closed his eyes and tried to visualize something with one eye and a long tail. He just couldn't make it work. He bit his lip while he thought.

"I know!" shouted Frances Kelly. "A needle and thread!" Everyone laughed. Frances was an expert seamstress. In fact, she had not one but two sewing machines, purchased in a year that the catch had been particularly good. The second machine was for her daughters, Marion and Dorothy; Frances wanted to teach them the craft of sewing. It was handy for an outport woman to be able to cut down old clothes to make new ones for her family. It was no wonder that she'd been able to come up with the answer.

Just then, the door opened, letting in a blast of cold air from outdoors. It was Mr. Inkpen at last. Everyone hurried to make him room. Grandma Hillier gave up her prized rocking chair to the storyteller and squeezed onto the daybed with her grandchildren. A hot toddy was pressed into Mr. Inkpen's hand. Everyone settled in. Moms sat on chairs around the kitchen table, the men stood by the stove and the kids piled onto the daybed.

Mr. Inkpen wrapped his crooked hands around the

toddy. He peered up from under his bushy grey eye-brows. "Why so quiet? What kind of a party is this? What ya all waiting for?" He gave a grin.

The children cried out, "A story, a story. Give us a story!"

"Well, then," replied Mr. Inkpen. "If it's a story you want…"

CHAPTER 4
When Wishing Still Helped

"ONCE UPON A TIME WHEN WISHING STILL helped, there was a boy. And he was called..."

"JACK!" all the children shouted. All the stories were about Jack; everybody knew that.

"Now, Jack, when he was just a little tyke, his parents got drownded. So Jack gets sent to live with his old Granny. And Granny was real happy for the company, but how's she going feed the little tyke? She's got no one to fish for her, and two mouths to feed. So Granny teaches Jack to jig. Then she sends him down to the sea every day to jig for cod. And while they don't have sugar or tea or none o' them fine stuffs that the rich folk have, they do all right, Jack and his Granny."

"As it happened there's a king lives right down the footpath. And he's got a daughter, the princess."

Murphy and Martin grinned at each other. There was always a princess.

"She's lonely and wants to get married but the king doesn't want her to leave him so he sets a contest. The man who can stop the wicked northwest wind from blowing will win his daughter."

Mr. Inkpen eyeballed his audience. "Can it be done?" The crowd shouted back, "No!" Mr. Inkpen shook his head skeptically. "Well," he says, "there was one who thought it could."

"Jack hates that cruel northwest wind. Their house has lots of holes in it, see, and that wicked northwest wind blows through every hole and crack and near freezes him and his Granny to death. They got no axe to cut any wood to fix it up, just a hammer, and a hammer by itself ain't much use. So Jack figures it's worth his while to stop that wind blowin' through all the cracks. He'd be warm and get a princess to boot. So he says to his Granny, 'I'm goin' to stop the wind. I'll find it, and stuff an old rag in its mouth and stop it from blowin'.' But his Granny, she says to Jack, 'Don't be a durn fool, boy. Nobody can stop the wind!' But Jack he doesn't listen. He goes down to his fishin' spot to think."

"Now there he is, fishin' and thinkin', and what does Jack do but catch himself a fine codfish, biggest codfish he ever saw. Now that fish could feed him and Granny the whole winter through! But just as he's bringin' it in, the cod opens its mouth and starts to talk!"

Martin dug his elbow into Murphy's ribs. A talking fish! This would be good.

"The fish says, 'Boy, let me go. I got a wife and seventeen babies down under. Let me go and I'll grant you a wish. I got the power.' Now Jack thinks to himself, 'A talkin' fish. Hmmm. Maybe he does got the magic.' 'Okay,' says Jack. 'This here's my wish. Stop the northwest wind from blowin'.' If a codfish could look surprised, this one would've. 'Dang, boy, don't be daft. It can't be done! Don't ya want a boat or a stage or somethin' reasonable?' 'Nope,' replies Jack. 'I want the wind stopped.' If a codfish could sigh, this one would've. 'I'll see what I can do.' And off it swims. Minutes later it was back, draggin' an old cloth. 'Here,' says the fish. 'This is better than stoppin' the wind. Lay out the cloth and watch.' So Jack lays out the cloth on the beach and the fish says, 'Spread, cloth, spread.' And like magic all Jack's favourite foods are on the cloth. 'Well,' says Jack, 'that's not stoppin' the wind but it's pretty fine. I'll take that to my Granny.' And off goes Jack."

"Jack's granny is pleased as punch with the cloth. Now she's got tea and cake, just like the rich folks. But Jack still wants to stop the wind. So he goes back down to his fishin' spot and doesn't he catch the same old codfish! And the codfish says, 'Not you again! Let me go, and I'll bring you somethin' nice. Not that wind thing, but somethin' nice.' But Jack says he still wants the wind stopped. The codfish shakes its head and swims away. A little while later he comes back and says, 'Go home. There's a hen runnin' around your garden. Take that hen inside and say, 'Lay, hen, lay.' She'll lay ya a golden egg. Then you can stop your fishin' and leave me alone.' So Jack goes home and finds the hen. And his Granny is even better pleased. But Jack, well, you know Jack. He wants what he wants."

"Next day, he catches that old codfish again, and this time the cod floats him an old piece of driftwood. 'Take this home, and say, 'Cut, wood, cut.' And forget about that wind, boy.' So Jack goes home with the wood and tries it out. That piece of wood turns into an axe and before you can say 'Gee willikers!' there's a whole pile of lumber at Jack's back door. Jack looks at that lumber and gets to thinkin'. Then he takes that wood and mends his house. Pretty soon there ain't a single hole, and no wind comin' through. 'There ya go, Granny,' says Jack. 'I done stopped the wind. I'm off to get the princess.' And all his old Granny could do was shake her head."

Mr. Inkpen looked around at his audience. "Jack be pretty smart, don't ya think?" he asked with a smile. "No, he's silly!" shouted all the children. Even the moms and dads were smiling. "You just wait and see," said Mr. Inkpen and got himself back into the story.

"Jack marches up to the king's palace and says he's stopped the wind. Now of course the king don't believe him. There's all kinds of wind blowing this way and that all around the palace. 'That's right odd,' muses Jack. 'Ain't no wind at my house.' So the king and the princess and all the court troop down to Jack's house to see. And inside Jack's house there ain't no wind, just like he said. But outside it's all around. And the king says, 'You're a fool, boy!' and Jack shrugs his shoulders. Just then his Granny invites the king for a bite to eat, because that's what you do even when your grandson's been called a fool. And the king sits down and Granny spreads the cloth and says, 'Spread, cloth, spread.' And all kinds of wonderful food appear. The king's eyes get real big. Then Granny says, 'Cut, wood, cut' and all kinds of firewood flies in through the window and stokes up the fire. The king's eyes get bigger. Then she says, 'Lay, hen, lay' and the hen lays a golden egg. She gives the egg to the king as a present, and asks him to forgive her foolish grandson. The king's eyes nearly pop out of his head. 'Forgive him?' he cries. 'I'm givin' him my daughter.'"

Everybody in Mrs. Hillier's kitchen cheered. Good old Jack had done it again.

"And I was there at the wedding," Mr. Inkpen went on. "It lasted for eight days and eight nights, each one better than the last. And I'd be there still, except I came here to tell you the story."

The crowd clapped and cheered. It was a very satisfactory story, that was for sure. Mr. Inkpen refused another toddy, saying it was time to make his way home. Goodbyes were said, then the mothers started serving up the night lunch.

Murphy, Martin and some of their soccer buddies took their lunches to a warm corner of the kitchen and sat down on the floor. "Hey, Murph, you could use one of them magic axes to build yourself a stage, couldn't you?" asked Ben. All the boys knew about Murphy's plans. They just didn't know he'd already started, and he wasn't about to tell them. "I could at that," laughed Murphy. "Who'll you pick for your princess?" Isadore said slyly. "Ya gets a house, ya gotta have one of them too! Bet you'll pick Annie!" All the boys snickered, even Murphy. "My house is for my mom. I don't need no princess! But those stories aren't real anyway. I ain't heard of any talking codfish around here!" All the boys laughed out loud.

"Hey, I got a story that's real," said Charlie. "I heard it from a sailor that came in on one of the schooners. Want to hear?" Of course they did. The boys scrunched closer together.

"So there's this schooner, right? And the first mate goes to the captain's cabin to ask him something and there's a man sitting at the captain's desk who's not the captain. He's not anybody the sailor knows! Nobody on board that ship, that's for sure. And so the sailor asks him what he's doing there. And the man looks up at him but doesn't say a word. Then the man picks up a slate and writes NORTH BY NORTHWEST on it. He hands it to the sailor. The sailor asks him what he means but the man doesn't write anything else. So the sailor leaves and upstairs he finds the captain at the wheel. And he tells the captain that there's a man, a stranger, down in his cabin. And that's a worry, so the two of them go back down but the man is gone. But the writing is still on the slate. And the sailor asks the captain if that's his writing and the captain says no. Then he writes the same words below to compare. NORTH BY NORTHWEST. The writing's not the same. The sailor and the captain just stare at each other. What does it mean? They both go back to their work, but the captain keeps thinking. Finally he turns the wheel north by northwest. He doesn't know why, but he does. And in no time he hears a call from the watch, 'Trouble ahead!' And dead ahead is a big fishing boat, jammed up on an iceberg, splitting apart. Fishermen are tumbling into the freezing sea, so the schooner captain gets the rescue boats out and saves every last man just before the fishing boat sinks. And while they're giving all the fishermen a hot drink, the sailor who saw the stranger comes up to the captain and says, 'That man over there?' He points. 'That's the man was in your cabin!' So the captain asks the man what happened. And the fisherman says he's never been on the schooner before. So they make him write the words NORTH BY NORTHWEST. And the writing's exactly the same as on the slate!"

The boys whistled. "And you say that's true?" asked Martin. "You sure?"

"That's what the sailor said," replied Charlie. "That's all I can say."

"I got one too," said Isadore. The boys turned eagerly towards him. "This one for sure is true, because my dad said he heard it from four different people who were there. It happened to a sealing boat. There's this father, see, and for the first time he's taking his son out on the ice. And the kid wants to do well so he works real hard. But one day all of a sudden his dad drops stone dead. His heart or something. So the kid's really upset and stops working. Then he changes his mind, cause he remembers that without his dad he's the only provider for his family. So then he works ten times as hard. The other sealers are impressed. They say his dad would be proud. The kid keeps working. One day he's out on an ice floe chasing the seals and he stays too long and a big storm comes up. There's snow blowing every which way and he can't see where he's going. The kid gets lost. He's out in the storm a long time and finally he lies down on the ice to go to sleep. He knows it's the end for him. Just then he sees this man coming across the ice. The man comes right up to him and says, 'Get up!' The kid gets up and it's his father! His father starts out across the ice and the boy follows him and pretty soon he sees the sealing boat. All the men are looking over the side at the boy. 'We thought we'd lost you!' they say. 'Who was that man with you? We can't find him.' And so the kid says it was his dad, his dead father, and that was the story all the other sealers told. They swear it's true."

The boys were silent. It wasn't hard to believe. The outport people lived at the mercy of the elements and death was never far away. The idea that your loved ones looked out for you after death was comforting. Murphy couldn't help but wonder if his dad would watch over him when he started fishing, just like the dad in Isadore's story. Maybe Noah had been dead too long? Did time matter to a ghost?

"Boys, the women are packing up the food. If you want seconds, you'd better hurry!" called out Isadore's dad. As one, the boys scrambled up and hurried to the kitchen table to finish off the last crumbs. Not even a ghost could stop a hungry boy. But Murphy was thoughtful. Was there any truth to the story? Was his dad out there somewhere, waiting for him?

That night Murphy had a hard time sleeping. His dreams were loud in his head, full of images tumbling about. Wooden axes cutting wood by themselves, people appearing and disappearing, fish talking to ghosts, cakes popping out of tablecloths, directions appearing magically on slates; a wicked northwest wind was blowing them about his brain and he couldn't make it stop.

Finally, Murphy got up. He lit a candle and opened his scribbler. Maybe if he finished the letter to his mom it would clear his head.

CHAPTER 5
Bella

BELLA LET MURPHY'S LETTER DROP INTO HER lap. She didn't know whether to laugh or cry. Being so far away from her son was hard, the hardest thing she had ever done. She knew in her heart that she had done the right thing to leave him behind, but it didn't help the loneliness. He had a good life in the outport, just as his father had wanted for him. And Murphy loved it; he wanted no other life. His letters made that very clear.

Bella shook her head at his description of cut-throating, in all its gory detail. Not that she needed a reminder. She had grown up in the outport too, and worked in the stage with her family, just like Murphy. It was impossible to forget the squelch of the guts, the pop of the heads, the writhing of the crawling maggots in the corners of the stage if you missed just a little bit of fish when you cleaned up. In the city she had to wear gloves all the time because her hands still bore the scars of the sharp knives. She all too clearly remembered the sting of salt in the wounds.

It wasn't an easy life, but it was a good life, filled with family and tuned to the rhythm of the seasons. Bella hadn't wanted to leave but she'd had no choice. Without a man to fish for the family, a woman could not survive alone in an outport. And the city was no place for a baby, so she had to leave Murphy too.

Bella arrived in St. John's with a tiny amount of paper money, borrowed from Randall's Bible, to help her start out. Her education in the outport, such as it was, hadn't prepared her for work in the city. Nobody in St. John's needed a good cut-throat. So Bella had to go back to school, even though she was a grown woman. She'd learned to work a telegraph, memorizing Morse code, practicing every night in her small rented room. In time, her Morse was fast enough to get her a job in the telegraph office. Bella was able to pay Randall back his paper money and move to a nicer room. But she was lonely.

Bella missed her son every single day. Each spring when she took passage on a schooner to visit Murphy for his birthday, she wanted to do nothing more than hold him tight and never let go. Of course, he was too big now to enjoy being hugged. A single tear rolled down her cheek. Murphy must miss her too. Imagine him wanting to build her a house! But each spring she was happier and happier to return to St. John's. That was her home now. Could she go back to life in the outport?

In truth, Bella had never considered moving back. Too much time had passed. Her life in the city was not the one she had chosen, but it was hers now. And Murphy had his. Secretly, she had hoped that he would want to move to the city some day, but she knew now that would never happen. He was his father's son.

Next spring, she would have to talk to Murphy.

Just then, Cora Dalton swept into the drawing room. "Whatever has happened, my dear?" she asked solicitously. "Did you receive bad news from home?"

Bella smiled as she quickly wiped the tear from her cheek. "No, Mrs. Dalton," she replied. "My son wrote to tell me about a party he has just attended. The fishing season has officially ended, and the families all got together for a bit of a time. Murphy is quite interested in riddles, you see, but he's just terrible at guessing the answers. His young friend Annie is much better, and he's clearly put out at being bested by a mere girl!"

Mrs. Dalton laughed. "A typical male, then, wouldn't you say, dear? How old is your son now?"

"He'll be thirteen next spring, ma'am," answered Bella.

"Such a big boy! And at what age do they begin to go out in the dories?"

"Murphy has been pestering his uncle all summer to let him go. Randall will probably relent next season. Most boys start in their early teens. Randall's quite careful, you see, because, well...because of what happened to my husband." Bella looked down at her lap. "Murphy seems to have gotten the idea that his father's ghost will watch out for him when he goes fishing, and so all will be well. Boys and ghost stories!" Bella laughed nervously. "Where do they get these ideas?"

"It is dangerous work. Do not begrudge him this comfort. And who are we to say that our dear departed do not look out for us?" Mrs. Dalton gently patted Bella's hands. "You are very brave, to give your son to the sea."

Two more tears ran down Bella's cheeks. "It is the lot of an outport woman," she said quietly. "And I shall always be one, whether I am there or not."

Mrs. Dalton shook her head in sympathy. "Yes, dear, I know exactly how you feel."

Bella smiled. Of course she did. Mrs. Dalton was married to Captain Vince Dalton; she too had to give up her man to the sea. A woman's lot was a hard one.

"On that note, shall we ring for tea?" Mrs. Dalton said brightly. "No point stewing over that we cannot change."

"Tea would be lovely," replied Bella. But it wouldn't stop the stewing. How could she tell Murphy she was not prepared to move back to the outport? Bella gazed around Mrs. Dalton's lovely drawing room. She felt very lucky to have a room in such a nice home. Mrs. Dalton had taken her as a boarder because, as captain of the schooner S.S. *Meigle,* her husband was absent for long periods of time. Mrs. Dalton got lonely in the big house, and Bella was perfect company. The two of them could sit in the drawing room on an evening over a cup of tea and do their needlepoint or listen to the radio together. Bella appreciated the company as well. Mrs. Dalton moved in society. She knew many people and often had musical gatherings and small dinner parties, to which Bella was always invited. Bella had met many interesting people. This was one of the reasons she felt she could never go back to outport life. Here, Bella was never cold, never wet, and no one smelled of fish.

"Tell me, dear, about these 'kitchen parties,'" said Mrs. Dalton, when the tea was served. "I've heard they are quite lively affairs."

"Oh my, yes," laughed Bella. "In the outports, everybody practically lives in the kitchen. Anybody's kitchen, yours, your neighbour's...no one knocks because kitchens are public spaces as far as outport folk are concerned. So when people feel like visiting, it always happens in the kitchen. Imagine, Mrs. Dalton, all your friends trooping into the house through your kitchen door, not knocking but just coming right in."

Mrs. Dalton looked suitably horrified.

"Everybody's wearing their gumboots, because that's what we wear. And you don't take them off because the floors are bare wood and your feet would freeze. So things get a little muddy."

Mrs. Dalton laughed. "My housekeeper would be appalled!"

"Not in the outports. Getting together is more important than a little dirt. Nobody's invited; everybody just comes. And there's no real planning, because the folks that come bring food and music with them. There are fiddles and squeezeboxes and ugly sticks and sometimes even drums to make the music."

"Ugly sticks?!" cried Mrs. Dalton.

"Absolutely," replied Bella with a smile. "And we sing and step dance and tell riddles and stories. The children run around until they fall in a heap on the daybed; the old folks get the few chairs and will often nod off in the midst of it all. And when everybody's tired we eat a night lunch and go home happy. That's a kitchen party, Mrs. Dalton."

"You make it sound appealing, dear," said Mrs. Dalton, "but I'm trying to imagine all those people crowded in such a small space, and the mud, and the noise…"

"You would love it, Mrs. Dalton," said Bella earnestly. "There is an honesty about the people that is sometimes lacking here in the city." Oops. Bella bit her tongue. That probably wasn't the proper thing to say.

Mrs. Dalton looked thoughtful. "Perhaps," she mused. "Bella, will you go back? When you talk about the outport, it sounds like you miss it."

Bella shook her head sadly. She picked up the letter in her lap. "My son writes that he is anxious for a share of the catch so that he can build me a house. So I can come home. It makes my heart sing that he wants to do that. But I can't go back. Not now. Not even for Murphy. And I don't know how to tell him."

There was nothing to say to that. The two women sat quietly drinking their tea, each deep in thought. All of a sudden there was a commotion at the door, then the sound of the maid murmuring, "Good evening, Captain." Captain Dalton had come home! His wife leapt up with a smile on her face and went to the hall to greet him. Bella followed more slowly. After a polite hello, Bella went upstairs to her room, leaving them to catch up in private.

In her hand, she held tightly to her letter, her son.

CHAPTER 6
A Terrible Roar

THE DAY AFTER A KITCHEN PARTY WAS USUALLY pretty quiet in the outport, what with people being tired from staying up so late and all. Murphy slept right through the start of school. Now that was good planning! If he could just get some brewis, or maybe a leftover lassie bun, and get out without Aunt Rosie seeing…

"Murphy!"

Murphy sighed. It never worked. "Yes, Aunt Rosie?"

"I'm thinking it's a beautiful day to get the washing done. Since you've conveniently missed school, will ya bring in some firewood and get the stove nice and hot? There's a good lad. Fiona, dear, what a surprise; you've missed school too! So go bring in some water. Take the hoop."

Ugh. Washing days were the worst. All day long, hauling water and fetching firewood to keep the wash water on the boil. Why was it that Aunt Rosie never took a day off? School was starting to look good. Murphy took a bun in one hand and the wood sling in another. Truly, he'd rather be fishing. Fiona gave a sigh that was very big for someone only eight years old and followed him out. She grabbed the wooden hoop just outside the kitchen door and slipped it over her head and round her waist. Then she picked up two buckets, holding the hoop and a bucket in each hand. The hoop was handy; it helped Fiona hold the buckets out from her dress so it didn't get splashed.

By midday Aunt Rosie's arms were red from the lye soap and her fingers raw from the scrub board. Her temper was in about the same state. Murphy offered to take the freshly washed clothes out back to hang on the clothesline. He knew Aunt Rosie found that to be heavy job.

"Well, all right, but mind you don't drag them through the dirt! I'll have your hide for that!"

Murphy smiled. Aunt Rosie was funny when she got all flustered and tired. She'd never taken his hide yet, although she'd promised a million times. He took the basket of clothes and hoisted it under his arm. Annie was waiting for him in the yard.

"Can we go to the headland now?" she asked. "You said we'd go!"

"Okay, okay," said Murphy. "Take it easy. I'll go if you stop yelling! But not now. I said *later.* We'll go after supper. I'm going to play soccer when I'm done with the washing."

"But you promise?" demanded Annie. "You really promise?"

"Yeah, I promise," Murphy sighed. "I'll meet you there after supper."

By the time he'd pinned the clothes to the line, Aunt Rosie had put away the scrub board.

"Well done, you lot. Off with you before I think of something else for you to do!"

Murphy raced off to Martin's house. Hardly any of the fellows had gone to school that day, so soccer was definitely on. On his way to The Gut Murphy collected Isadore and Charlie and Thomas and Ben. Martin and his brother Albert joined the group and they all went tearing off to The Pond. The Pond was shallow and pretty boggy, but past the bog was a nice flat meadow, just right for soccer. Within minutes the ball was in play, and the lot of them ran like fiends. Morning chores were long forgotten.

After a while, the boys called the game a draw and fell down in a heap in the meadow.

"Ground feels cold," said Isadore idly. "There'll be weather soon."

Nobody answered. Then Albert piped up, "Me dad's going to the cards tonight. He's lettin' Martin and me come. Anybody else?" Boys were allowed to stand behind the men and look at the cards so they could learn how to play.

"There's going to be cards? I bet Rory's going. He likes to play cards more than he likes to do anything. More than fishing even, these days. I'll ask my aunt if I can go too," said Murphy, forgetting completely about his promise to Annie.

"Don't think so, Murph," said Charlie. "I saw him after lunch, headin' out in the dory."

Murphy was surprised. Rory avoided the boat and the sea as much as he could. What was he doing?

"Where was he headed?" asked Murphy curiously.

Charlie exchanged a glance with Martin. "He was going to St. Pierre, looked like."

Murphy caught his breath. St. Pierre! That was a little island just off the peninsula. It didn't belong to Newfoundland; it belonged to France. Hardly anybody spoke English over there. Lots of families had friends and relatives on St. Pierre, but not Murphy's family. The only other reason to go there was to buy alcohol, hard liquor. What was Rory thinking?

Murphy looked at Charlie in disbelief. All the guys were staring at their shoes. Everybody knew but him.

"I heard Rory's goin' to the city. Soon as the fish are in," said Charlie. "That true, Murph?" The other boys nodded. They'd heard it too.

Murphy was shocked. Shocked about Rory and shocked he didn't know. How could it be true if Rory's own family didn't know? Murphy felt like a dumb cluck.

"Uncle Randall'll never let him go," replied Murphy breezily. "We're fishermen, after all." That was safe enough to say, Murphy was pretty sure. Rory had to be crazy to think about going to the city. You only did that if you had to, like his mom. And if Uncle Randall caught Rory drinking...there would be a fight for sure.

Thomas changed the subject. "Well, I can't go to the cards," he said. "My mum and dad are takin' the footpath to the next outport for the Orange Lodge meeting. My mum baked a blueberry pie. I got to stay home and babysit."

"Yeah, me too," added Ben. "There's a whole lot of 'em going to the Lodge meetin'."

"Not my dad," said Charlie. "He's already gone back in the bush to cut firewood. Won't be back till next week."

"Same as my uncle Randall," Murphy absently nodded in agreement. He was still thinking about Rory.

Charlie jumped up, grabbing the soccer ball. "Shall we have another go?" he asked. Then he dropped the ball and fell down.

The rest of the boys started. The ground was shaking. Really shaking, right under their backsides. It had shaken Charlie right off his feet. The soccer ball was bouncing, all by itself. Eyes wide, they looked at one another. Murphy rolled to his knees, but didn't try standing. The grass in the meadow was shivering. Murphy felt like he was riding on the back of some great beast, feeling its energy through his hands and knees. The beast was in control, not him. He didn't like the feeling. And it seemed to go on and on, that shaking. Minutes, anyway. It felt like a long time.

Then it stopped, just as suddenly as it had began.

"Whew!" breathed Martin. "What *was* that?"

The boys looked at one another. "I never felt nothin' like that!" exclaimed Ben. Gingerly, he stood up. "Ground's solid now."

All the boys got up. They looked at the soccer ball. It lay quietly. "Do you think it were ghosts?" asked Albert in a whisper. "Evil spirits, mad at us for some-thin'?"

All the boys had ghosts in their heads after the storytelling. "Ya think?" asked Martin. Murphy thought for a moment. "Nah," he said. "Can't be ghosts. Ghosts are like air; they fly around on the wind. They don't hide inside the earth, shakin' every-thing silly. Right?" The rest of the boys weren't so sure.

"But their bodies are in the earth. Maybe it's ghosts tryin' to escape into the air?" suggested Ben.

"Not the right time of year," said Charlie firmly. "They can only escape on All Saint's Day. Ain't that right?"

Albert persisted. "If ghosts tryin' to escape their graves make the earth shake, then what about ghosts tryin' to escape the sea? You know the ones that drown in the ocean like Murphy's dad? Do they make the sea shake?"

"I don't know," replied Murphy. He had a much gentler image of his father's ghost, and he didn't think it would make all that scary shaking happen, on land or sea. "Maybe it wasn't ghosts. Maybe it was an explosion, far away like. Do ya think?"

The group thought about that for a minute.

"Maybe," said Martin. "Yeah, well. I'm thinkin' Albert and I better go on home and check on Grandad. He's poorly, you know, and he might be feelin' nervous. Gotta go, guys."

"Good idea," said Thomas bravely. "I oughta check on my family too." As one, the boys struck out on the footpath that led back to the village. They'd hardly gone any way at all when they met Mrs. Moulton running along the path.

"My sheep!" she cried. "They've run away!" Then she was gone, apron askew, hair escaping from her kerchief in every direction.

"I guess we weren't the only ones to feel it," said Charlie.

By the time they got back to the village, the boys could see that everyone, young and old, was congregating on the wooden footpaths that linked the stages. Everybody was talking about the shake. It was a ghost, it was an explosion, it was the new factory up the peninsula starting its equipment, it was a storm coming – everybody had an idea. The only thing for sure was that nobody had felt the like before. Nobody but Old Antoine.

"*C'était un tremblement de terre* – earthquake," he said loudly to the assembled crowd. "That's what it was, *tout exact.*"

"Are you sure?" asked Mrs. Rennie. "We don't get earthquakes around here, not ever."

"*C'est vrai*, it is true," retorted Old Antoine. "I feel them before." Old Antoine got down on his hands and knees and put his ear to the ground. Ben started to snicker.

"*Oui*," said Old Antoine as he laboriously got to his feet. "The tidal wave next. That's what." Old Antoine dusted off his trousers.

"What did you hear?" asked Isadore curiously.

"*Rien*. Nothing."

Isadore frowned.

"*Écoutez*," said the old man. "Not what I hear, what I feel. *Je suis vieux*; I been around lot of years and before my back get crooked I been lot of places. Places with the tidal wave. The wave – vibration – go through my ear to my head. Feel it before; feel it now. *Écoutez* Old Antoine."

The assembled grown-ups looked at one another in embarrassment. Old Antoine got such funny ideas sometimes.

"Old Antoine," said one of the old-timers in the crowd kindly. "Just look at the harbour. It's flat as a mirror. No waves, no wind, no weather. We won't be getting any waves today."

"*Si vous aimez*. Believe what you like," said Old Antoine firmly. "*Moi* – I go to the high ground."

Old Antoine turned on his heel and stalked away. The crowd began to murmur. "Do you think he's right?" asked somebody. "Should I take my children to the high meadow?"

Another voice answered, "Don't give it another thought. You know Old Antoine; he's such a worrier. A day doesn't go by that he doesn't predict some disaster or another. Sure, they get tidal waves in some places, but we ain't never had one here. Not to worry. Go home everybody, make your dinners and put your little ones to bed. It's all over now."

Murphy nodded to his friends as they split up to go their separate ways. He wasn't convinced. What was a tidal wave anyway? Was it the sea shaking? Was Albert right – were ghosts to blame? He was still wondering when he got back to his house, only to find a great commotion.

Sean was crying, Fiona was shrieking and Aunt Rosie was trying to settle the whole crew down. The minute he came through the door, Fiona grabbed him.

"Ember bit Sean!" she cried. "Ember bit Sean! Oh, I can't believe it! He wasn't doing nothing, just feedin' him a carrot like he always does and then Ember bit Sean!"

Murphy shrugged her off. "Give it a rest, Fiona," he said. "You make my ears hurt! Quiet down and tell me slowly. What happened?" Aunt Rosie gave Murphy a grateful look. Murphy took Fiona into the tiny parlour so Aunt Rosie could concentrate on the weeping Sean.

"Start again," he commanded.

"Well, it's like I said," hiccupped Fiona. "We were just up at the meadow feeding the animals. I had to milk the cow, see? And Sean was givin' Ember his carrot – Ember loves carrots! – and then all of a sudden Ember bites Sean! And then, right after that, the ground started to shake and I thought a monster hand was goin' come up through the earth and grab Ember and punish him for doin' such a bad thing!" Fiona stopped for breath. "It was real scary, Murphy," she went on. "Do you think Ember's a demon? Have we got evil spirits on the loose?" Fiona clutched Murphy's arm. "I'm so scared!"

Murphy untangled his arm and rolled his eyes. "Calm down, Fiona! It wasn't any evil spirit. It was just an earthquake." Murphy was quite pleased that he had heard the discussion down on the footpath. Now he could sound right smart. It was way better than feeling like a dumb cluck.

"It's a natural kind of thing that just happens sometimes. Ember probably felt it coming and got scared just like you did. So he did something he doesn't usually do. We all do funny stuff when we're scared. It wasn't really Ember's fault." Murphy felt like a schoolteacher. He wasn't completely sure that what he was saying was correct, but it made more sense to him than angry ghosts and demon horses. And Fiona was settling down – that was the main thing.

"You think?" she asked. "Ember's not possessed?"

"Nope," replied Murphy firmly. "Just scared. Now that the earthquake is over, he'll be back to his old self. You'll see." Fiona gave a little smile. Murphy decided not to mention the possible tidal wave, an idea that was still niggling at the back of his brain. Nah, that was nothing. Old Antoine was just, well, Old Antoine.

"Okay, Murphy," said Fiona. "I'll go tell Sean he's not to worry, okay?"

"Go ahead," smiled Murphy. Kids these days. Good thing he was practically a man.

"CAN I GO WATCH THE CARDS TONIGHT AT MR. Walsh's, Aunt Rosie?" asked Murphy.

"I suppose," she replied. "I guess that's where Rory is. Haven't seen him all day. With your uncle Randall back in the bush cutting wood there's no need for a big supper. Eat something first. Don't be late home."

Murphy grabbed a cold supper, then made his way to the cards. He was anxious to go, anxious to get away from Aunt Rosie so he didn't have to answer any questions about Rory. Murphy felt upset and uncomfortable. Sure Rory was unhappy, but that would pass. He shouldn't be making decisions when he was unhappy, Murphy decided. They were bound to be bad ones. He just hoped Rory would make it back before bedtime, or there really would be trouble.

As he walked along the footpath, Murphy could see lanterns bobbing along the high path, the one that led to the next outport. Must be the folks on their way to the Lodge meeting, he thought. He could pick out young Mr. and Mrs. Hillier, the ones who had hosted the kitchen party, and the Hipditchs as well. He saw old Mr. Hillier, too, going in the opposite direction. He was probably going to the Temperance meeting, the one where they sat around all night talking about the evils of alcohol. Lots of folks made fun of Mr. Hillier for that. He could hear sewing machines cranking away as he walked by the Kelly house. That made him remember the riddling from the kitchen party. Mr. Bartlett waved to him as he walked by. Mr. Bartlett was just closing up the mercantile store. He'd probably be going to the cards too, once he'd had his supper. The footpath began to angle up the hill. Murphy was nearly there.

A warm light, soft murmurings and explosions of laughter were coming from Prosper Walsh's house. The game was in full swing. Murphy nodded to Martin as he walked into the kitchen. The boys tried to stay kind of quiet in the presence of the men. Fly on the wall, fly on the wall. Mr. Walsh won a hand.

The next game was a close one. Finally Mr. Rennie won, to great cheers from everybody. "Well played, well played!" they shouted. Martin was grinning all over his face, proud of his dad. As the next hand was dealt, the men got to talking about the earthquake.

"Odd thing, that," said one. "The west coast has earthquakes all the time. But not us here on the east coast. It's an odd thing indeed."

"You're right about that," replied another. "Did you hear the crazy story Old Antoine's been spouting? Now that we've had an earthquake, we're going to have a tidal wave too! Have you ever heard the like?"

Prosper Walsh went still. "What did you say?"

"Old Antoine's predicting a tidal wave," the men repeated. "Says it'll come because of the earthquake. Put his ear to the ground and everything!" The other men guffawed. But not Mr. Walsh.

"That's not funny," he said seriously. "I've seen one of them tidal waves. Down in the south, when I was working on a schooner crew. They call them 'tsunamis' there. Does Old Antoine really think the earthquake's going to set one off?"

"That's what he says. He thinks he can feel it in his head!" said Mr. Rennie. "But Prosper, look at the harbour! It's like a mirror, still as glass. Don't fret yourself."

But Mr. Walsh stood up, scattering his cards. "We've got to get the women to high ground," he said. "We've got to do it right now."

"Calm yourself, Prosper!" said Mr. Brushett. "There'll be no wave tonight. Deal the cards."

But Mr. Walsh left. They could hear him run next door and start hollering. The other men shook their heads and went back to the game. Murphy nodded to Martin from across the room. He pointed his head at the door. The two boys sidled out.

"Whaddya think?" asked Murphy. "Who's right?"

"Darned if I know," replied Martin. "Would it hurt to go to high ground, just in case?"

"I don't think so," said Murphy quietly. "I'm going home."

"Me, too," said Martin. But just then his dad called him inside. Murphy waited outside the open door. He watched his friend lean down and whisper in his dad's ear. He saw Mr. Rennie frown and shake his head. Martin looked towards the door and shrugged. Murphy shrugged back in reply and started to make his way down the footpath alone.

Surely it would be all right. Mr. Brushett knew the waters around here as well as anybody. If he said there wouldn't be a tidal wave, than there wouldn't be. But

Murphy had a sick feeling in his stomach just the same. The men said they never got earthquakes either, and they'd got one. As he hurried along the path, Murphy heard an odd sound. He stopped. It sounded like poor, sickly Mr. Chester slurping broth through a paper straw. Outside, in the dark? Something wasn't right. It was a sucking sound, to be sure, but it was growing louder and louder. More like a giant sucking the sea dry than Mr. Chester sucking his soup. Murphy looked around in confusion. Where was the sound coming from? It felt like it was all around him, and it was so loud now it filled the night. The sick feeling in his stomach got worse. Something was really, really wrong. But what?

The sucking noise stopped. All was quiet again. Murphy started walking again, more cautiously this time. He glanced towards the harbour. He looked again, peering into the dark. He stopped dead. He blinked and looked again. The water in the harbour was gone.

Now, that just couldn't be. A whole harbour full of water can't just disappear. But by the light of the moon Murphy could see that all the dories were tipped on their sides, just lying on the empty seabed. Their chains were clanking as the boats rocked from side to side, no longer supported by water. Where did it all go?

Murphy's heart began to pound and he started running. He had just reached the little white fence that enclosed their garden when he heard the sound again. Not sucking this time. It was a noise like nothing he had ever heard before: the greatest, the loudest roar of all time. It was the water, and it was coming back.

Murphy looked up in horror. A sixty-foot wave was racing down the harbour, crushing stages and throwing dories high into the air. It was heading straight for his house. He leapt over the fence.

Bursting through the door, he threw Sean over his shoulder, grabbed Aunt Rosie's arm and screamed at Fiona. "Run!" He hauled Aunt Rosie out the door. She was too startled to protest. They had barely stepped onto the porch when freezing water started to lap around their ankles. Aunt Rosie saw the water and went into instant action. She grabbed Sean down from Murphy's shoulder and started to pull him uphill while shouting over her shoulder at Murphy to "Get her! Get her!"

Murphy dashed back into the house. He was wet to the knees. Fiona was looking around in confusion. Murphy grabbed her and pulled her out the door. "You're hurting me!" she cried. Murphy didn't care. "Where's the water coming from?"

Murphy didn't bother answering. He just ran, pulling his cousin after him. How high would the water go? Could they outrun the wave?

CHAPTER 7
Run!

THE ROAR OF THE WATER COULD BE HEARD for miles. The men at the card game looked up in surprise. The folks at the Orange Lodge meeting stopped eating pie. The leader of the Temperance Meeting ceased his sermon and cupped his hand to his ear.

What was it?

As one, all of them rushed outside to see what was the matter.

MRS. RENNIE HAD JUST COME DOWNSTAIRS AFTER putting four-year-old Margaret to bed. She sat down at her sewing machine. All of a sudden icy water was swirling around her waist.

Dorothy Kelly was sewing too. Just pillowcases, but her mother told her that as soon as she could sew a straight line she could try some harder projects. When she heard the noise, she looked up at her mother, then over to the kitchen door. Her sister Marion was standing on the porch. Marion grabbed their baby brother Elroy, who was three, and ran away. Why was she doing that? Then Dorothy felt the house start to move beneath her.

Mrs. Brushett put two of her girls to bed. Pearl was tired and Lillian had the earache. Mrs. Brushett wondered if she should call Nurse Cherry. Minutes later, she was waking the girls. The older children in the family were pushing Pearl and Lillian into their winter coats. "I'm sick!" cried Lillian. "Why do I have to get up?" "Hang on to the bedposts!" their mother cried, as the house lifted from its foundations and headed out to sea. The house stayed perfectly upright the whole time. It sailed all the way to a nearby island then it stopped. The wave disappeared. Before anyone could react, a second wave picked up the house and sent it back where it had come from. The second wave disappeared, leaving the house close to where it used to be.

Grandma Hillier was having a pleasant evening. She was babysitting her three youngest grandchildren while their parents were at the Orange Lodge meeting. An older granddaughter, Irene, had come to play with the little ones as well, and they were all having a lovely time until frigid water began to pour into the house.

Uncle Chesley Hillier was babysitting the rest of the Hillier grandchildren at their house. A responsible uncle, he was supervising their homework when Ruby looked outside the window. "What's that, Uncle Chesley?" Chesley looked out the window. Chesley blinked. It couldn't be. But it was. There were white-caps outside the window. Heavy, rolling waves where they had no business being. Chesley grabbed the baby and pushed the rest of the children out the door. "Run to the church, fast as you can," he cried.

Old Mr. and Mrs. Inkpen heard the noise and went out to their porch. "This doesn't look good, dear," said Mr. Inkpen. "We'd best get moving," she agreed. Carefully the two old people stepped onto their wooden flake to cross over to the footpath, but as they did the flake broke from its frame and launched itself into the harbour. Clutching the makeshift raft, the couple held on tightly. "Not to worry," said Mrs. Inkpen. "Look, our neighbours have seen us!" and true enough, there were waves and shouts from shore. The couple waved back, just as the fragile flake broke in two, throwing both of them into the icy water.

"My house!" cried Mr. Rennie. The card players watched in horror as the Rennie home was picked up by the wave and launched down the harbour. Then it stopped, and swirled. The water under it began to recede, then a second wave, forty feet high, picked it up again. The house literally flew back towards land, where it was thrown up into the air, landing with a splash in the middle of The Pond. The second wave receded, leaving everything quiet, still and dark.

The people at the Lodge meeting stared in disbelief as the water ran out of the harbour and then pummelled its way back in. One wave, a second wave, then finally a third rocked the harbour, destroying everything in its path. Then all was still. Nan and Herbert Hillier and David and Jessie Hipditch stared at one another.

"What about our village? What about our harbour? What about our *children*?!"

As one, the four raced back to the footpath and began to pick their way back to their own outport. Any time the path dipped low, the path disappeared. The little wooden bridges that connected sections of the path were splintered or gone all together. Cautiously they made their way home, their fears growing as distraught people passed them along the way, shouting and crying.

Old Mr. Hillier staggered down the path from the Temperance meeting. He felt disoriented and confused. He'd gone home to check on his wife, but he couldn't find the house. Where had she gone? Where had the *house* gone?

MURPHY'S FEET WERE COLD. He'd lost his gumboots. Aunt Rosie would have his hide for sure this time.

They were his only shoes. He couldn't remember when he'd lost them exactly. He thought maybe the first one had come off when he jumped the fence. The second one, well, he just didn't know. Maybe when the wave knocked Fiona and him off their feet it sucked his boot off at the same time. He'd tried to hang on to her but the wave kept pushing him. It was hard to breathe. And it was so cold. He lost Fiona too. It was all he could do to keep his head above water. Especially when the wave started to drag him down towards the harbour. It was going back to the sea and taking him with it. Murphy flailed about, trying to grab onto something, anything. His foot caught. He wasn't sure on what, but he grabbed for it and hung on. He felt the water disappear from beneath him as the water went back to where it came from. Murphy gripped his support even harder. Was he dead yet? Was Fiona?

Murphy's foot was caught in the clothesline. He was clutching the pole that held up the line and all around him was strewn Aunt Rosie's washing, soaking wet and filthy dirty. Oh, she was going to be so mad! Murphy unwrapped his foot and looked around. Their house was gone. The storage shed with all their food was gone. All the houses that used to be nearby were gone. But somehow, the dirty washing seemed to be the worst thing of all.

"Murphy!" Murphy started. He was so cold, he could hardly think. Who was that?

"Murphy, over here!" It was Fiona! She was caught in the clothesline too. Murphy crawled over to her and started to untangle the knots that had captured her. His fingers just didn't seem to be working right.

"RUN! RUN!" Murphy and Fiona looked up. Everything seemed to be moving in slow motion; it was like they were sleeping. Who was shouting? Why all the urgency? Then Murphy heard a roar. The wave was coming back.

Adrenaline surged through his veins. Yanking the last of the clothesline from Fiona's leg, he grabbed her hand and pulled her to her feet. As they ran up the hill, Murphy looked back over his shoulder. A second wave was racing towards them, even deadlier than the first. This one was smaller, but it carried with it all the debris from the first wave. Murphy saw somebody's roof, chunks of firewood, even a dead sheep roiling up the hill towards them. They weren't going to make it this time.

MARY ANN AND ELIZABETH WALSH HEARD THE ROAR of the wave as they sat with their knitting in their rockers. Both in their eighties, they had seen and heard much in their lives but never anything like this. They looked at one another in dismay. There was a sense about the commotion that felt dire. But at their great age, they couldn't run away. Mary Ann reached out and took Elizabeth's hand. The house began to break up around them. Mary Ann was wrenched away. Elizabeth, alone, closed her eyes and began to pray.

"HURRY!" FIONA TRIPPED. Murphy kept running, dragging her to her feet. Higher, higher, they had to get higher. Aunt Rosie, holding onto Sean above them, kept shrieking at the top of her lungs. "RUN! RUN!" Well, they were doing their best. The wave was nipping at their heels like a naughty dog. Then it stopped. The wave stopped. It reached its crest and started to roll back down the hill towards the harbour where it belonged. Murphy fell to his knees. He and Fiona crawled the last few yards to Aunt Rosie. She pulled the pair of them into her arms. Then they heard another roar.

Ready to run once more, the four of them watched the water rise. The third wave was much smaller than the first two. It tossed the wreckage of the village about, broke the houses into even smaller pieces and hurled their belongings even further out to sea. It left silence in its wake. The roar of the water had been so loud it left a thrumming in their ears, as if the water had gone right inside their heads. Was it over?

Cries and shouts began to break the stillness. Those above looked in horror at what lay below. The entire outport was a mess of splintered wood and broken dories. The few low-lying houses that hadn't disappeared completely were sitting askew and tilted on their foundations or crushed to kindling. Once again, the water in the harbour was still. But now it was a mass of floating debris. Clothes, cabbages, barrels of molasses, kegs of salt and lumps of coal were tangled in the mess of splintered wood floating in the water. And fish – there were dead fish everywhere. The entire catch was gone.

NOBODY SAID ANYTHING. What was there to say? Their outport had disappeared.

Who was gone? Who was left?
What was gone? *What* was left?
Whatever were they going to do?

MURPHY WAS SHIVERING. The questions were too big, too scary. Nobody in the world could answer them. They had no place to live, no food to eat and no clothes but the wet ones on their backs. Not even a pair of gumboots to wear. It was dark. It was cold.

Then the north wind picked up and it started to snow.

CHAPTER 8
A Little Shake

B ELLA WAS JUST GETTING READY TO GO HOME for supper when the earth began to shake. She grabbed the desk and held on, looking around her in confusion. What was happening? The other workers at the office looked just as confused. It was the oddest sensation, a sort of rolling or rippling that rose up through the ground into her toes and made her feel dizzy. A picture fell off the wall, the glass shattering into a thousand pieces. Bella looked up at the ceiling apprehensively. Should they run outside? Was the roof going to come down on their heads?

Before she could reach a decision on the question the shaking stopped. The leaves on the plant she had on her desk kept shivering for a few more moments. Finally, everything went still. There was nervous laughter in the office. "Well, that was interesting!" said one fellow. "I've never felt an earthquake before."

Earthquake! But this was the east coast. Only the west coast had earthquakes, wasn't that true? Bella hoped that Captain Dalton would be home for supper. He was a worldly man, having sailed to all four corners of the globe. Surely he would know all about earthquakes. Bella tidied up the broken glass before she left the office. It wouldn't do for someone to get hurt.

The servants at the Dalton home were a-twitter when she arrived home. "Miss!" they cried. "Did you feel it? Did you feel it?" She smiled and nodded yes.

"An earthquake, I've been told," Bella said.

"The sugar crock fell off the table! It cracked in half. You should have seen Cook scurry! The sugar was dancing up and down but still Cook tried to scoop it up, moaning about the ants it would bring. It's November! There ain't no ants in November!"

Bella smiled. "Was there anyone hurt? Any other damage?" But no one knew.

Captain Dalton was late for supper. "My apologies, ladies," he said. "I made a trip to the harbour to check the schooner. The earthquake was not likely to do any damage to a ship in water, but I felt I should be sure."

"And was everything all right?" asked Mrs. Dalton.

"Oh yes, my dear," her husband replied. "Just as I suspected. You'd never know anything had happened. Across town, the word is that other than a bit of broken crockery, there's no damage anywhere. That earthquake came simply to give us a little excitement at the end of our day!" The ladies laughed politely. Bella thought she could have done without that little bit of excitement herself, but as long as there was no harm done it was no never mind. She wondered if Murphy had felt the shaking. With his current interest in the supernatural, he probably thought ghosts were to blame! She would have loved to see his face when the shaking began. He was a brave boy so he probably wasn't afraid, just curious. He and his friends would delight in telling stories about it.

The talk at supper moved on to other things. Black Tuesday in New York was still very much in the news and it was affecting trade everywhere. Nobody had any money to buy goods any more. Many men were losing their jobs. Once again, Bella was grateful her son had security at the outport. There would always be codfish.

After dinner, a gathering was planned in the drawing room. Bella was not particularly looking forward to it for it was in honour of Sir Richard Squires, the Prime Minister of Newfoundland. Politics had never been her cup of tea. And now, with the stock market crash and money being tight everywhere, the topics for discussion were even more limited than usual. Money, money, money. Who has it and where to get it. It was all rather tedious. She'd have much preferred a musical evening herself. But it would be rude not to attend, so after dinner she went upstairs to change her dress.

Next morning, Bella arrived early at the telegraph office. The earthquake, minor as it was, had upset her and she had slept badly. She was anxious to see the news and reassure herself that it hadn't done any damage anywhere else. But to her surprise, there was no news. The earthquake had broken several underwater telegraph cables, so many areas of the Dominion had lost their connection to St. John's. Bella's worries grew. What did that mean? Was it simply a communication issue, or were the broken cables part of a bigger problem?

The other workers at the telegraph office assured Bella that all was well. Those areas that still had telegraph connections reported no damage. The coastal areas where the outports were located had limited communications even in the best of times; it was not the least bit unusual for their cables to be down. There was simply no reason to be alarmed. All day Bella worried and all day positive reports came in. Finally, even she came to believe that all was well at the coast. Her boy was fine.

CHAPTER 9
Good News and Bad

MURPHY WAS FREEZING. THEY ALL WERE. Their clothes were soaked with icy seawater and the ground beneath them was cold with frost. Fiona was weeping, held tightly in Aunt Rosie's arms. Murphy looked up at the sky. Snowflakes caught on his eyelashes. He had no idea what to do next.

"I want my coat," sobbed Fiona. Murphy looked down the hill. Fiona's coat and every other thing they owned were gone. Annie's house next door was gone too. Where were they? Murphy could see lanterns begin to bob along the edge of the harbour below them. But he couldn't hear anything. All that was in his head was the great roar of the tsunami. That terrible noise drowned out everything else. The snow was falling, soft on the ground. It was like a blanket. Yes, a blanket would be nice. Maybe if they just stayed where they were, huddled together, everything would be all right...

"Rosie! Rosie!" came a shout. "Are you all right?"

It was Uncle Randall, slipping and sliding down the hill from the forest. "Ach, Rosie! When I felt the shaking I started for home to make sure you were all right. I didn't expect this!" He pulled his wife into his arms. "You're all right, you're all right!"

"'Twas Murphy," whispered Aunt Rosie. She was shaking her head in disbelief. "Runs in like a madman, grabbing Sean, grabbing me, yelling at Fiona. We'd never have made it otherwise." Aunt Rosie was shaking like a leaf. "What a terrible thing," she sighed, and closed her eyes. "What did we do to deserve this?"

Uncle Randall held his wife tightly in his arms. He caught Murphy's eye. "Good man," he mouthed. "Thank you."

Murphy shrugged his shoulders. Finally Uncle Randall calls him a man and all he wants is to be a kid.

"Where's Rory? Is he all right?" asked Aunt Rosie. "Murphy, was he at the cards?"

Murphy didn't want to be in charge of this problem. It was too big, too confusing, especially on top of everything else. "He's gone to St. Pierre," he blurted out.

Aunt Rosie gasped. Uncle Randall's face went quiet, stonelike. His lips went thin. Then he looked at the rest of his family. "We've got to get you dry and warm," he said briskly. "I'm taking you to the church. Come on."

Uncle Randall took Sean and Fiona by the hand and Murphy took Aunt Rosie's arm. They followed Uncle Randall up the hill. It was full on dark now, but the moon reflected a bit on the snow and that helped. Still, it was hard to see rocks and roots and that made for slow going. Slowly they picked their way up and over the meadow, heading towards the patch of light filtering through the stained glass windows of the church. Murphy took a quick glance around. Other than the lanterns down at the harbour, there were only six patches of light. One of them was the church. So there were five houses left, out of seventeen. He tried not to think about what that meant.

The closer they got to the light, the louder the roaring in Murphy's head got. Now there were people noises mixed in with the roar. But they weren't good sounds. Murphy stuck his fingers in his ears. He wanted to scoop out all that sound and throw it away. But it wasn't like a ball of wax. The noise was stuck.

The light inside the church was terribly bright on the eyes after the dark outside. And the smells weren't much better. The place was stuffed full of people, too many for Murphy to count. A whole bunch of kids were sitting together near the nave, most of them wet and pretty stinky. There were some moms crying by the stove in the back. Somebody had put a kettle on the stove to make hot tea and was handing it out to everybody, but a pot of tea doesn't go far when there's that many. And there weren't enough cups. They had to share. All the men not off in the bush were gone, probably holding up those lanterns down by the harbour. Sean and Fiona found their friends in the pile of kids and sat down quietly with them. All the kids looked pretty bewildered. Aunt Rosie went straight to the stove. The other women reached out their arms and embraced her. Uncle Randall turned to leave.

Murphy grabbed his arm. "Where are you going? Can I come?" Uncle Randall started to shake his head. "Please," pleaded Murphy. "I can't stay here!"

Uncle Randall took a quick glance around at the women and children then looked back at Murphy.

"I guess you can't," he admitted. "But you're not going to like what's out there. You sure?"

Murphy nodded his head vigorously. " I gotta move," he said. "I gotta do something."

"Come on then," said his uncle. They headed outside. Just below them was a cluster of lanterns. "We'll go see if they need help."

The lanterns were perched on what was left of the Inkpen's stage. About a hundred feet from shore was the silhouette of a dory. Murphy's heart seized. Where was Mr. Inkpen, the storyteller? His house was all broken up and he was old. Had he washed out to sea?

The men on the shore were getting ready to haul the incoming dory up on shore when it arrived. Murphy waited, his heart pounding. The lantern light showed a circle of debris floating in the water. Caught up in it Murphy saw three gumboots, a coat and a baby. His heart nearly stopped in horror and he jumped. But it was only a doll.

"Ho there," came the call. Murphy got ready. The dory scratched up on the beach and the men worked together to pull it high. Mr. and Mrs. Inkpen were in the dory! They were okay! Pretty wet, but alive.

"My, my," said Mrs. Inkpen as Murphy helped her out of the boat. "That was a swim all right. I'm grateful to you boys for coming to get us."

"No trouble, Missus," replied one of her rescuers. "It's just a lucky thing we saw you out there in the dark."

"That's the God's truth," agreed Mr. Inkpen. "There wouldn't be a hot toddy nearby, would there now?"

Murphy had to smile. Good old Mr. Inkpen. "There's hot tea at the church," he offered. "Will that do?"

Mrs. Inkpen nodded. Her teeth were starting to chatter and she was shivering. She was an old woman and a winter swim in the waters off Newfoundland wasn't smart for anybody. "Murphy, take the Inkpens up to the church," ordered Uncle Randall. Murphy nodded.

Up the hill they went, slowly, slowly. Murphy could see that the Inkpens were failing. The cold, the wet and their age all combined were getting to them. He tried to make them hurry, telling them how warm the church was and all. Finally they got there. The minute they came through the door the women took charge, hustling Mrs. Inkpen off to the side to get her into dry clothes, wrapping a blanket round Mr. Inkpen. Murphy sighed. They'd be okay now.

Murphy headed back down the hill to the harbour. He could see the lanterns of the men that were checking the shoreline. They were over by the Brushett house now. Murphy squinted. He thought it was the Brushett house. But it wasn't in quite the right place. Close, but not exactly. Was it just the dark playing tricks on him?

Murphy joined the men. Mr. Hollett, the magistrate for the peninsula and the closest thing they had to a government official, was talking.

"Amazing thing," he said. "The wave picked up the house and floated it out to sea. It sailed as straight and true as the finest schooner! We saw it go all the way out to the island, stop and settle down. Then the second wave came, picked it up and floated it right back, nice as you please. I've never seen the like!" The magistrate was incredulous. "I couldn't believe my eyes!"

His wife was wringing her hands. "Those poor children!" she wailed. "Five children in that house, oh my!"

Just then there was a shout. "Hey there! We're up here! Can you help us down?"

The group looked up in amazement. Mrs. Brushett stuck her head out the upstairs window. Alongside it popped five more, smaller, heads.

"We're stuck. We can't get down," she hollered. "Anybody got a ladder?"

The group on the ground stood speechless.

BUT IT WASN'T ALL GOOD NEWS. It wasn't just the houses that were gone. Some people hadn't had time to get out before the wave hit. It had come so quickly. The Hilliers were the hardest hit. The home of Grandma Hillier was washed out to sea. Inside had been Grandma Hillier, her three youngest grandchildren and her older granddaughter Irene. They were all gone with the house. The house of the younger Hilliers was still standing and the distraught relatives had gathered there to mourn their terrible loss. Murphy could hear moaning and weeping coming from the house. It sure made losing your house and all your food and all your clothes in the middle of winter seem hardly bad at all.

Uncle Randall called out to Murphy. "Come on," he said. "We need to help your friend Martin. That family's in trouble." Murphy frowned. They were all in trouble, as far as he could tell. Why was Martin's worse?

It was pretty easy to see once he and the other men got to The Pond. The Rennie house was floating in the middle of it, bobbing gently up and down in the shallow water. Mr. Rennie was kneeling by the side of The Pond, holding his head in his hands and weeping. Martin and Albert were standing behind him like statues.

"My wife!" Mr. Rennie cried. "My family!"

Uncle Randall and a couple of the other men hauled one of the few remaining boats over to The Pond. It was hard work. Leaving Mr. Rennie on the shore, they rowed to the floating house. Carefully, gently they pulled out Mrs. Rennie and her younger children. They were drowned. Drowned when the house made its wild rush out to sea on the crest of the first wave. Sadly, the men rowed back.

Albert cried. Martin didn't, but Murphy could tell he wanted to. Murphy didn't know what to do. Should he say something? Should he yell swear words at the wave, now gone back to sea? Would it help to have something to blame? Should he put his arm around Martin, to show him he felt bad too? Should he cry, so that Martin could? Murphy didn't know. He didn't know anything.

"Margaret, where's Margaret? Where's my baby?" cried Mr. Rennie. His wife and younger children had been laid on the ground at the edge of The Pond and Mr. Rennie was holding his wife's cold hand. He began to look around frantically. "Margaret! She's not here! Where's Margaret?"

The other men began to talk quietly amongst themselves. Murphy went to stand close to the men so he could hear. "Do you think the baby floated out to sea?" asked one of them. "Should we drag the boat back to the harbour and search for her?" "Maybe she's at the bottom of The Pond," said another.

Martin spoke up. He'd come over to the group of men too. "My mom would have put her to bed. In her cot, upstairs. She'll be in the cot. You've got to find her cot." Martin looked sadly over at his father. "You've got to find her."

Uncle Randall eyeballed the house. "It's still afloat. If the cot is upstairs, we may tip the house trying to get to the second story."

"We'll have to sink it," replied one of the other men. "We'll need another dory. We'll row it over to the house, push it inside then fill it with water. That'll sink the house, give us access to the top floor. What do you think?" The other men discussed the details, then agreed it might work. It sounded pretty complicated to Murphy. Murphy and Martin both went with the men to haul another dory out of the wreckage of the harbour and drag it to The Pond. This one was broken up pretty badly but all it had to do was survive one trip to the middle of The Pond. It was hard work but they did it. The boys watched from shore as the men rowed the two dories to the floating house.

The boys couldn't see much in the dark. The shadow of the house did seem to shrink, so maybe the plan was working. Murphy still didn't know what to say to his friend.

After what seemed a long time a single dory started to grow large. The men were coming back. Murphy saw his friend clench his fists. This was going to be hard. Margaret was a baby. It just wasn't fair. But then Murphy heard shouts coming from the dory.

"She's alive, she's alive!" Martin's eyes grew large and Mr. Rennie jumped to his feet. "She's alive!"

Murphy turned to Martin. "It was your idea to look upstairs. You saved her, Martin," he said solemnly. "You saved your sister."

CHAPTER 10
Annie

THEY TOOK MARGARET BACK TO THE CHURCH. She was a mucky duck for sure, all covered in mud and seaweed. But the whole outport wanted to cheer. She was alive. Alive!

Murphy was happy to see that Aunt Rosie didn't look so white any more. Having some chores to do always made her feel better; the worse things became the busier she wanted to be. Well, thought Murphy, she could sure keep busy in the church. At the moment, Aunt Rosie was conferring with Mrs. Walsh about how to make the small store of tea last the evening. The moms seem to think it important that everyone had a hot drink. Warm 'em up, that's the ticket. That's all we need for tonight. Maybe they were right. He didn't want to think about tomorrow either.

"Murphy!" No question, that was Aunt Rosie hollering. Maybe she thought everybody would feel better if they had chores? "Go find us some dry wood for the stove, will you? We want to keep everybody warm. And Murphy," she said more quietly, just to him. "Have you seen Rory yet?"

"No, ma'am," Murphy said. Why had Rory picked this night to be an idiot? Murphy headed outside. Actually, it did feel good to have a chore. It helped make the roaring stop. Murphy opened the door to head outside only to be pushed aside by Annie's mom.

"Where is she?" she screamed. "Where's my Annie?" She caught sight of Murphy and grabbed him by the shoulders. "You know where she is! She said she was going with you. You promised to meet her; she had to go. Where's my Annie? Where IS SHE?"

Murphy was flummoxed. The woman was crazy. What was she talking about?

"Annie, Annie! Tell me where she is!"

All of a sudden, Murphy remembered. That morning, when he was helping Aunt Rosie with the washing, he'd promised to meet Annie after supper. They were going to go to the headland. She had something to show him. He promised. Then forgot all about it. The men were playing cards; he wanted to be with the men. He was worried about Rory. He completely forgot. And Annie didn't.

All talk in the church stopped. Everybody was listening.

"Is your daughter missing?" asked somebody. "Do you think the wave took her?"

"No, nooooooo!" cried Annie's mom, sinking onto a pew. "Not the wave! She just went off, said she had to meet Murphy. Murphy, please, where IS she?"

Just then Annie's father rushed in. "I can't find her anywhere!" he cried. "Boy? Do you know where she is?"

The roar in his head was getting louder. Murphy couldn't think. Annie, Annie. He'd promised! But it was okay. Wasn't it? If she'd gone to wait for him, she'd be on the ledge, where their shelter was. It was protected. It was high above the wave. Murphy was sure about that. Pretty sure, anyway. Annie was probably okay, but trapped. The only footpath to the headland started in the high meadow, but dipped down low. There was a wooden footbridge to cross, then the path headed high again. If Annie had been at the headland, she wouldn't be able to get back because the wave had surely taken the footbridge. She was stuck out there all by herself. Safe, but alone.

Murphy bit his lip. What if the ledge wasn't high enough? What if she'd been caught out on the rocks? What if she wasn't okay? It would be all his fault because he forgot his promise.

Murphy didn't think about the fact that because he forgot he'd been able to save his aunt and cousins.

All he could think about was Annie. She'd been waiting for him and he hadn't come.

"I know where she is," he said to Annie's mom, to all the people in the church. "I'll go get her."

Voices erupted from all sides. *Where is she? You can't go get her! It's dark; the footpaths are dangerous. Murphy, where is she? How do you know? Where IS she?*

He took a big breath. He looked at Aunt Rosie. He looked at Annie's mom. He closed his eyes, then opened them.

"I promised I'd meet Annie at the headland after supper. I went to the cards instead. I think she's probably on the ledge, halfway up the hill in a shelter we built. She can't get back because the footbridge is gone. I'll go get her."

Once again, the voices erupted. He was too young; a grownup should go. Nobody should go; it was too dangerous. Annie was eleven; if she had a shelter she'd be fine until morning. Everybody was firing questions at Murphy. How protected is the spot? How good is your shelter? Could she wait until morning? They'd send a search party then. Everybody had an idea, but Murphy knew what he had to do. He had to get Annie. That's where he should have been all along.

"I'm going," said Murphy firmly, to no one in particular. All conversation stopped.

"I'm going. It's my fault she's there. I'm the only one who knows where she'll be," Murphy said again.

"I'm going."

"All right then," said a voice. There was silence, then heads began to nod all around. It was what a man ought to do.

Prosper Walsh said, "Best to take him by water. There are search parties still looking for folk. Murphy can go with them and get dropped off at the headland. Can you find her from there, boy?"

Murphy said he could. And so it was decided. "Take a blanket," said Aunt Rosie, pushing the one she had wrapped around her shoulders into his hands. "She'll be cold."

"You'll need something on your feet. Does anybody have any gumboots?" said another voice. Boots were handed through the crowd. "Dry socks? Anybody?" But there were no dry socks. Not a single pair. Everybody was wet.

Before he knew it, Murphy was sitting in a dory holding the blanket. The men were telling him not to be afraid. He wasn't, not of the dark, not of the cold, not of the snow, not of the prospect of climbing the headland in too-big boots. He was only afraid that he might not find Annie, but he couldn't put that thought into words.

It took a long time to get to the headland by water. There was so much debris in the harbour they had to use a stick to push it out of the way in some places. Three times the dory detoured to check a

house or a shed that had been moved or crushed by
the wave. They found old Elizabeth Walsh. Murphy
had always wanted to see a dead body. He remembered Mr. Inkpen's words from the storytelling. *"In the
days when wishing still helped..."* Now he wished he'd
never seen one. He wished he'd remembered Annie.
He wished Rory wanted to be a fisherman. He
wished there'd never been a big wave. But these were
not the days when wishing still helped. This was real.
Finally the dory reached the end of the harbour. The
men pulled it up sideways along the shoreline and
Murphy scrambled out.

"Give the lad a lantern," said one of the men.
"When you find her, flash three times. We'll be
waiting. But hurry. The tide's going out and the wind's
picking up. If you take too long we may not be able
to hold against the current. We'll have to go back. If
we have to leave you, we'll flash just once. Take shelter
and we'll come back for you in the morning. Have
you got that?" Murphy nodded.

"Be careful, boy," called out one of the men.
Murphy waved them off. With half an eye he noticed
that the dory had pulled up right where Annie and
him had tied together his stage. Except the stage
was gone.

Murphy didn't want to light the lantern just in
case one of the men mistook his message. It wasn't
much use in the swirling snow anyway. But the rocks

were slippery. Generally when a rock was wet it looked black, and you knew to be careful on that one. But everything was black as far as Murphy could tell. So every step had to be careful. Slowly he climbed up the rocky headland. She'd be on the ledge. The ledge should be off to his right. He was pretty sure.

It was hard going. There was nothing to hold on to and out there on the headland Murphy was completely exposed. The wind was so much stronger than in the village and the snow was blowing in his eyes. He couldn't really tell where he was going. Where was the ledge?

"Annie!" yelled Murphy. "ANNIE! Where are you?" He had to find her quickly, or the men would leave him there.

The wind caught his words and tossed them into the sea. This was a dumb idea, Murphy finally decided. If Aunt Rosie knew how bad the wind was out here she'd have his hide, for real this time. He was going to be blown right off the rocks and into the ocean, all while Annie was sitting all comfy up on that ledge, away from the wind. What a stupid idea this was!

"Annie!"

If he built his house here he'd have to blast out a path down these rocks. And put in a railing, that's for sure. Murphy looked down. He hadn't actually come very far. He looked up. The snow was swirling everywhere and it made him feel dizzy. He had no idea where the ledge was. Off to the right or off to the left? Left, thought Murphy. Definitely left. But just then he saw a glow. Just a little one, off to the right. Was that the ledge? Did Annie have a lantern? Murphy blinked. The glow had moved a bit farther to the right. He decided to go right.

Up and over, up and over. The glow was leading him to the far side of the headland and that was good because the wind wasn't as strong. The glow got stronger. Murphy peered through the storm. The ledge was just ahead, he was sure of it! Just like that, the glow disappeared. Clever Annie! She'd led him straight to her hiding spot.

"Annie! Annie! Are you there?" Finally, Murphy heard an answering call. He climbed the last few steps and there she was, curled up in a tight ball, hidden in their shelter. Murphy's stomach unclenched with relief. Girl or not, Annie was his friend. Murphy scrambled up beside her and sat down.

"I brought a blanket," he said. "Here." Annie wrapped it around herself and hugged herself tight. She sucked on her braid while she looked at him.

"You're late, Murphy," she said.

Murphy was dumbfounded. He looked at Annie. Then they both started to laugh. But the laughter only lasted a minute before Annie's eyes welled up with tears.

"How bad is it?" she asked. "I saw everything. I was just sitting here waiting and you didn't come and I was getting mad and it started to get dark and I was just about to leave when the water disappeared. I couldn't believe it so I waited and watched. From here I could see the wave coming from the sea." Annie started to cry in earnest.

"I jumped up and down and yelled and everything but nobody heard me! I kept yelling and yelling. Then the wave came." Annie hugged herself under the blanket. "I saw the whole thing," she repeated in a whisper. "I saw everything."

Murphy didn't know what to say. He'd only caught a glimpse of the wave before he'd had to concentrate on running away from it. He guessed it must have been pretty awful to sit back and watch it tear the outport apart. For the second time that night, he didn't know what to say to a friend.

"I gotta signal the men in the dory." Murphy stood up abruptly. "They're waiting for us but the tide is going out and they can't wait too long. We have to hurry." Murphy carefully lit the lamp, then ventured out to the edge of the ledge where he knew the light could be seen. He held the lantern high. Then he turned around so that his body hid the light. He faced out again, then turned. One more time. Then he waited. Three flashes came back.

"It's okay," said Murphy as he came back out of the wind. "They got the signal and they're still waiting. But we gotta hurry, Annie."

Annie got to her feet, still clutching the blanket. It was harder going down. Murphy kept his lantern lit now that he'd given the signal, but it cast only a small circle of light. The snow was swirling harder and faster, distorting the shapes of the rocks. Away from the protection of the ledge, the wind sucked away their breath and threatened to push them off the rocks. Slowly, slowly, step by careful step, Murphy led the way down to the water.

They were only halfway there when Murphy saw another signal. One flash, one flash only. The men had left them.

Murphy led the way back up. "Don't worry, Annie," he said gently as they reached the ledge. "The men saw my signal so they'll be able to tell your mom you're all right. We'll stay here in our shelter; it'll be fun, right?"

Annie said nothing, but Murphy could hear more crying. He reckoned he'd better leave her alone until she sorted herself out. Girls and tears; well, he didn't think even grown men knew what to do about that. While he waited he crawled outside the shelter and collected snow to pack around the driftwood. He tried to pack it in all the cracks to keep out the wind. Murphy half smiled; he was just like Jack, trying to make the northwest wind stop blowing.

Annie took a couple more minutes to stop blubbing. Then she wiped her nose on her sleeve and said, "Thanks, Murphy. Why'd you come anyway?"

"I felt bad. I went to the cards instead," he replied.

"Did you forget about me?" she asked.

Murphy bit his lip. "Pretty much," he said finally.

Annie didn't say anything. Finally he heard her mumble, "Boys!" He guessed that was all the talking they'd do about that. Murphy heaved a sigh of relief. Annie gave him a lassie bun from her chipped plate. She'd brought a wee picnic and Murphy was starved. But he hardly wanted to eat it, thinking about all the hungry people in the church. Better not to say anything to Annie about that yet, or there might be more tears.

"So how bad is it in the village?" asked Annie.

"Pretty awful," replied Murphy.

"Anybody hurt?"

Usually Murphy liked to be the one with the news. But this news wasn't easy to tell. And telling it didn't make him feel good.

Annie cried some more when the telling was done. "Nothing's going to be the same, is it?" she asked.

"Nope," said Murphy.

"Are you going to forget about your house? Will you go to live with your mom in St. John's?"

"Nope," replied Murphy.

"She'll probably make you go after this," Annie mused. "I would, if I were your mom. I built you a flake."

"What?" exclaimed Murphy.

"That's what I wanted to show you. I built a flake. I even put one fish on it, for good luck. But it doesn't matter now. The wave took it."

"It took our stage too," said Murphy. "Go to sleep. Tomorrow's going to be a long day."

The two of them wrestled for a share of the blanket for a bit, then settled down to wait out the night. Murphy was exhausted. Was it was just last night that they were dancing up a storm in the Hillier's kitchen? That reminded Murphy of something.

"Hey Annie," he said, "You asleep?"

Annie mumbled something back.

"Just, I wanted to say thanks for leading me up the cliff with your lantern. If I hadn't seen that glow, I'd probably have gone off in the wrong direction."

"What lantern?" asked Annie sleepily. "I don't have a lantern."

"But I saw a light," repeated Murphy. "It led me around the headland to the ledge and that's when I found you."

"Maybe it was the moon," replied Annie. She curled up into a tighter ball under the blanket and went back to sleep.

Not Murphy. He was wide awake. That glow hadn't come from the moon; he knew that for sure. And it had stopped him from going the wrong way in the dark.

So what was it?

CHAPTER 11
Murphy's List

ANNIE HOGGED THE BLANKET ALL NIGHT. Murphy was cold and hardly got any sleep. He couldn't remember why he'd thought he couldn't wait until morning to look for her. Annie would have been just fine without him. Murphy sighed. He'd never have been able to sleep back at the church, not knowing if she was okay. And she'd clearly needed the blanket — all of it. Codwallopers, he was cold.

Murphy stood up and tried to work the crick from his back. The wind had really howled all night; it was practically a blizzard. But the snow had stopped, finally. He nudged Annie with his toe.

"Get up! Let's go home."

Annie groaned and held the blanket even tighter. "Leave me alone!" she grumbled. Murphy shook his head in disgust. He looked out over the harbour. The snow made things look a little better, but you could still tell that something was terribly wrong in the outport. There were hardly any houses, and most of the buildings that remained had big holes stove in their sides or collapsed roofs or were tilted off their foundations. Mr. Bartlett's store was still there. But there was something odd about it. Murphy stared. It was turned around. The store was just where it was supposed to be but the door was on the wrong side. That wasn't good. Bet most of his stuff was broken. Murphy wondered about the telegraph. It was in the store. If it was broken would they be able to call for help?

Annie finally stood up beside him. "Wow," she breathed. "That's pretty awful."

"Yeah," agreed Murphy. "We'd better get started down. The men will be back for us soon. There's going to be lots of chores today, that's for sure."

"Did you notice something, Murphy?" asked Annie.

"What?"

"Look at all the snow on the ledge."

"Yeah, so?"

"And there's no snow on the headland."

"No, so who cares?"

"Don't you see, Murphy?" Annie asked patiently. "This proves it. The ledge is protected from the wind. The snow didn't get blown away, even though it got blown off all the rocks. And building high was smart.

The shelter didn't get washed away. So this *is* a good place for your house, just like I said."

Murphy looked about. She was right. But it was kind of hard imagining building a house for himself now. Murphy shrugged and started to climb down to the water.

In no time at all a boat arrived to pick them up and row them back to the village. But it wasn't the dorymen. It was Rory.

"What on earth are you doing out here?" Rory shouted as he rowed to shore. Even from a distance he looked tired and grumpy.

"What on earth are you doing out *there*?" Murphy shouted back. He was furious. "Were you out all night? Don't you know what happened? Or were you too busy drinking to notice?"

Now Rory was angry. "That's none of your business, small fry," he said quietly. "And I don't know what you're talking about, only that you're way out here early in the morning and mom is going to be furious!"

"Aunt Rosie knows where *I* am," Murphy retorted. "It's just *you* she couldn't find when she needed you!"

"Why did she need me? Doesn't a fellow have a right to some time on his own?"

"Look," said Murphy, calming down a little. "That's why she needed you." Rory was working the oars. He had his back to the harbour. When Murphy pointed, he twisted around to look.

Despite the blanket of snow, everything looked worse by daylight. It was like a giant foot had stomped on the village, crushing everything in its path and knocking the rest askew. It didn't look like a place where anybody could live.

Rory gasped.

"It was a tsunami," explained Murphy. "Our house is gone. Everything is gone."

"Our house is gone, too," piped up Annie, who had been trying to make herself invisible while the boys were fighting.

Rory said nothing; he just stared. Then he went back to rowing, his jaw set.

They went straight to the church. Annie's mother screamed as soon as she saw her daughter. Aunt Rosie enveloped Murphy in a huge soft hug the minute he walked through the door. Then she hugged Rory as if all the worry he had caused was forgiven. Half of the village was inside the church, all jammed in together. The smell was awful. Seaweed and salt water and dead fish; even some of the animals that hadn't run away were inside the church. There wasn't any other place for them. The door to the priest's quarters was closed. That's where they'd laid out the bodies of the dead.

"Murphy!" The hug was over. Rory had gone to talk to Uncle Randall. Murphy didn't want to be a fly on the wall for *that* conversation. Aunt Rosie was back to doling out chores. "We need dry firewood. Get yourself something hot to drink, then go see what you can find, will you?"

Murphy went over to the church stove. The kettle was on the boil; it looked like it had been on the boil non-stop since last night. There wasn't anything to eat. He was grateful for Annie's lassie bun. Murphy pulled off his stiff socks and put them on the drying line for when he came back into the church. The gumboots were freezing, but at least he'd have something warm to wear later. After a weak cup of tea Murphy headed outdoors.

There was no shortage of wood to burn what with all the houses broken up and all; the trouble was finding anything dry. All that wood lying about and not one bit of it dry enough to burn. Murphy sighed. He'd have to head up to the forest, away from the harbour. Somewhere there had to be dry bark and dead twigs, enough kindling to keep a fire going long enough for the wet wood to catch. Murphy looked around for a piece of canvas to take up with him to pile the kindling on. With his feet as cold as they were, he only wanted to make one trip.

Murphy found a canvas sail amongst the debris. Maybe somebody had used it once to turn a dory into a sailboat. It would work. He dragged it up the hill towards the meadow, planning to head on to the forest. But before he got there he heard a holler.

"Ho there! Are you from the outport?" called a man's voice. Murphy turned to look.

"Hello!" Murphy shouted back. "Yes, I am."

In just a moment the group was upon him. Two men from a village up the peninsula were leading a horse that was piled with blankets and bundles. Murphy's mouth watered. He smelled bread! Sitting atop the pile was Nurse Cherry. Murphy grinned. Nurse Cherry didn't visit their outport much, but today was sure a good day for her to come.

"Were you hard hit, boy?" asked one of the men, named Albert. "Did the wave get you?"

Murphy nodded. "I think we got only five houses left in the village. We lost the whole catch and most of the cabbages. Almost all the boats and fishing gear. And..." Murphy didn't know how to say the last bit. "We got some people that's died. Nine or ten at least."

The other man, named Thomas, sucked in his breath. "That's bad. Worst we heard yet."

"Have you come to help, Nurse Cherry?" asked Murphy.

"Yes, dear," replied the nurse. "Alfred and Thomas here fetched up some food and blankets and things from our village. There wasn't much damage there. But we were thinking that you folks might be in a bad way; your location isn't as protected as ours. We thought we'd better come check."

"Thank you, Nurse Cherry," said Murphy politely. "I know for a fact Mr. and Mrs. Inkpen got washed out to sea. We collected 'em back but they were real wet and cold and they're pretty old. Maybe they need some medicine."

"Boy, I remember the day you were born," said Nurse Cherry. "Your mother told me your name meant 'sea warrior.' I'm guessing you never thought you'd have to fight the sea so hard."

"No, ma'am," replied Murphy sadly. "I think the wave won this battle."

He led the small party back down the hill. In no time they were making their way into the village. Murphy led the group towards the church.

"You'd best start here, Nurse Cherry," said Murphy. "The church is where most of the people went. And next go to the Hillier house. The house is still okay but the people inside got a terrible sorrow to deal with. But I don't suppose you got a medicine for that."

Inside the church, Nurse Cherry looked around in alarm. From every corner of the church she could hear coughing and hacking. The people had all been soaked through the night before, then assaulted by a blizzard, and they had no dry clothes, hardly any blankets and virtually no supplies. Some of them were clearly already sick. Looking around, she could also see signs of shock and exposure. If just one person got the flu or bronchitis, the rest would catch it in a minute. Nurse Cherry began to bustle.

From one knot of people to the next she moved, handing out what little food they had brought in their bundles and sharing out the blankets. She insisted those with wet clothes take them off and wrap themselves in blankets, and put the clothes on the drying lines tied near the stove. She gave the children hot water to warm them up. Some of them were already glassy-eyed with fever. She brewed herbs to soothe the coughs. She set broken fingers crushed by debris, stitched up cuts and rubbed salve on bruises. Nurse Cherry was a whirlwind. But even so, there was only so much she could do with the meager supplies available.

"Murphy!" the nurse called.

Aunt Rosie, who had been about to send him back outside for wood, instead pushed him in Nurse Cherry's direction. "Be a good lad; go help the nurse." Murphy went.

"We need to get these people warm," the nurse said urgently. "Can you light a fire outside? Collect some beach rocks and heat them in the fire. Then bring them in. Let people wrap them in their blankets, or put their feet on them, or hold them in their hands. Anything that will help get them warm. They need more clothes!"

"I'll do it, Nurse Cherry," said Murphy. "But I need to go to the forest for dry kindling. It'll take a bit of time. And we don't got extra clothes. The wave took 'em all." Nurse Cherry shook her head in dismay.

Building a fire was a good way for Murphy to keep warm, too. The search for dry firewood took him up to the forest and all over what was left of the outport. Some of the other kids came to help search; it was something to do. Annie came. It didn't matter any more that she was a girl; they all had to stick together. Even Martin came. He and Albert were staying with another family while their dad sorted out what to do next. Murphy's heart felt like a tiny piece of black coal, burning hot with anger at what that wave had done. Aunt Rosie was right. What *had* they done to deserve this?

Once they had a fire going strong, all the kids who weren't sick set out to look for some nice beach rocks to heat up for the people in the church. "This'll do, won't it, Murphy?" asked Sean.

"Sure, it'll be fine. Be careful; put the rock just at the edge of the fire."

Quietly, the kids collected rocks until the bonfire was ringed with them. Nobody felt like playing about. Annie poked at the stones with a branch, rolling them over to heat them through. When one was done, Annie rolled it into a bucket Murphy found, and one of the kids carried it into the church to warm up somebody's blanket. While they waited, Murphy and Martin sat on a log.

"You think you'll stay here?" asked Murphy.

"Dunno," replied Martin. "Dad doesn't know what to do. He doesn't want to stay but all he knows is fishing. Maybe we'll try another outport. Unless they're all wrecked like ours."

"You think they're all wrecked?"

"Depends on the wave. Who knows?"

"Martin, something weird happened last night," said Murphy slowly. Martin looked at him.

"I think I saw my dad," he went on.

Martin's eyes grew large. "You're joshing!"

Murphy told him about the glowing light. "You think it's like that story about the sealer? About how he saved his son?"

Martin was thoughtful. "I didn't really believe that story," he admitted. "But who knows?" The boys sat in silence for a while.

"And there's somethin' else," Murphy went on. "Annie and me, we were buildin' a stage out at the headland."

"I thought you said it was a bad idea!"

"I did. But she talked me into trying," Murphy replied sheepishly. "I only did it to stop her from buggin' me. But what was weird was that every time we needed something, like lumber, we just found it lying about. Almost like somebody left it for us. You think that could have been my dad too?"

Martin's eyes had grown very large. He was saved from offering an opinion on the strange events by the magistrate, Mr. Hollett.

"Boys!" he called. "Can you write? Can you count?"

"We're twelve!" said Murphy indignantly. "Of course we can!"

"Good then, come with me," said Mr. Hollett. "We need to take a tally."

They started at Mr. Bartlett's mercantile store. Murphy was amazed. The wave really had turned the store around. But nothing inside got broken. Everything was okay, just on the other side of the room. Because of that, it took awhile for Martin and him to find a pencil and a scribbler each. Their job was to follow Mr. Hollett around the outport from house to house, family to family, and keep a tally. Martin wrote down what people had left that they could share. It was Murphy's job to write down what the sea had stolen.

By the end of the day, Murphy's list was three times as long as Martin's. Still, Mr. Hollett said it was a good job done. He told them to report back to him early the next morning and they'd start sharing out what they could. "Boys," he said, "the telegraph line is broken. We can't get any messages out. We have to look after ourselves for a while, so we need to share things very carefully. It's an important job."

Murphy explained all this to Aunt Rosie later. She was impressed that the magistrate had chosen Murphy for the job. "Your mother was right all along!" she crowed. "She always said you were a smart one, that you'd go far."

Murphy shrugged. He still didn't see why that was important. "Mr. Hollett's going to write a letter to the Prime Minister, asking for help."

"Use a page of that scribbler to write a letter to your mom, too," reminded Aunt Rosie. "She'll be worried sick about you. Make sure you tell her you saved our lives!" Murphy grinned.

The next morning Murphy and Martin went down to Mr. Bartlett's store to get their instructions from Mr. Hollett. Rory was there too. Murphy glowered at him.

"Why are you here?" he asked his cousin rudely. "It's not like you care about what happens to the outport!"

"Stop being an idiot," Rory shot back. "Of course I care. I love this place as much as you. I'd just rather be on land than sea. So shut up!"

The three of them wrestled down a wheelbarrow from the upper meadow. They weren't sure who it used to belong to. Then they loaded it up according to Mr. Hollett's instructions. One house had cabbages to share; another had tea. One family hadn't lost any flour, so that mother baked bread all day long and the boys delivered the hot loaves to the church. Spare blankets were found and given to those who were sick. Once the dads had made sure that there were no more bodies floating in the harbour, the little kids were allowed to go down and rescue what they could. They found gumboots and pots and chairs and toys and bits and pieces of fishing gear. It all got laid out on the beach for sorting. By the end of the day, a dozen people who had lost their shoes were wearing boots. Including Murphy. He'd given back his borrowed boots and now had a pair that fit, sort of.

Nurse Cherry left with Albert and Thomas. She was exhausted but still worried about the other outports. So off they went down the coast to check in and lend a hand where they could. Some of the men made their way in from cutting firewood in the forest. They knew nothing of the disaster until they walked across the upper meadow and saw the destruction. The grieving started all over again.

By the third day, Murphy was exhausted. Everybody was. It was just so cold. They needed coats and mitts and hats. They needed houses. The ones they had left were bursting at the seams, overflowing with people. They were hungry. Why wasn't any help coming? Lots of the kids were sick, but there was nowhere for them to go but the church. It wasn't a nice place to be any more, especially with Nurse Cherry gone. Murphy tried to be anywhere else, which meant that most of the time he was outside trying to keep warm by a bonfire. So he was one of the first to see the schooner S.S. *Portia* sail into the harbour.

As the schooner fought its way through the floating debris, Murphy could see right away that it wasn't a rescue boat. He could tell from the looks on the crew's faces as they leaned over the rail staring at the harbour. Their faces were white with shock. The sailors were not prepared. They didn't know about the tsunami. Did that mean that nobody knew they were in trouble?

CHAPTER 12
The S.S. Meigle

T HE *Portia* HAD TO ANCHOR A LONG WAY OUT in the harbour because of all the debris. The captain and a half-dozen of the sailors rowed a lifeboat in to shore. Mr. Hollett was waiting.

"What happened here?" asked the captain, aghast, as he got out of the lifeboat. "We passed nine – nine! – buildings bobbing in the waves on our way into your harbour!"

"It was a tsunami," answered Mr. Hollett. "Our situation is very grave. We have many homeless and some families have lost loved ones. We have lost our food and our coal and our clothes. How is it with the other outports?"

"You are the first we've seen," replied the captain. "We were not expecting this. There have been no reports of damage from anywhere!"

"That must be because the telegraph is dead. We have been trying to send a message for three days. The other outports must be in the same predicament. Do you have a radio on board?"

Two of the sailors rowed Mr. Hollett back to the schooner to send a message. The captain and the other sailors remained on shore to survey the damage. It was hard to know where to look. There were great piles of splintered boards, useless for anything. There were empty spaces where houses used to be. There were no boats, no docks, no stages. And there were no people. It was as if the ones the waves had spared were afraid to come out.

Mr. Hollett had been writing letters to the Prime Minister of Newfoundland every day since the disaster, even though he had no way to send them. He decided that the telegraph message had to be brief; he would send the more detailed letters back with the captain of the *Portia*. He asked the radio operator to send his message direct to the Prime Minister.

"Tell Sir Squires this," Mr. Hollett began. "Two and one half hours after the earthquake an immense wave swept away all waterfront property. We have experienced serious loss of life and devastating property losses. Many are homeless, cold and hungry. There are likely similar losses up and down the south coast of the Burin Peninsula. Please send aid immediately."

Leaving the rest of his letters to be delivered by hand, Mr. Hollett was rowed back to shore. The captain of the *Portia* decided to return to St. John's immediately.

"There is no point in our canvassing the other outports for damage reports," the captain told the magistrate. "We have no way to give aid at this time. Better that we return to the city and come back properly prepared." Mr. Hollett agreed.

"Godspeed," he said sadly. The message was finally out. But the task ahead had just begun.

BELLA WAS BUSY WRITING YESTERDAY'S NEWS INTO the big book she kept when she heard her telegraph spring to life. Quickly she sat down, pencil ready, to take down the message. The crash of the stock market in the United States was causing all sorts of problems for their neighbours to the south and Bella wondered when the money troubles would begin to affect Newfoundland as well. But this message wasn't coming from the United States. It was coming from the S.S. *Portia*. Probably reporting in that her cargo had been delivered, Bella thought to herself. As the code was tapped out, Bella's pencil flew across the page, neatly taking down every letter. It wasn't until the brief message was complete that Bella looked down to read what she had transcribed.

Bella moaned as if she were in great pain. "Nooooooo!" she cried. The other telegraph operator looked up in surprise.

"What's wrong, Miss Bella?" he asked.

"My boy, my boy," Bella whispered. In surprise, the operator got up and took the message from Bella's hand. He read it and gasped. "We have to get this to the Prime Minister right away!" he shouted and ran from the room, leaving Bella weeping at her desk.

SIR RICHARD SQUIRES GOT THE MESSAGE JUST before noon. He sank down into the big leather chair behind his desk. "But it's winter!" he said. "And they have no houses?" He called his officials into his office. Together they decided that Captain Dalton's schooner, the S.S. *Meigle*, would become a rescue boat. Aides were dispatched to the Royal Storerooms and instructed to purchase flour, beef, sugar, tea, nails, blankets and all manner of other things that might be useful. Doctors and nurses volunteered to go to the stricken area. The *Meigle* was loaded. Captain Dalton only had time for a brief goodbye to his wife, Cora. He rushed home as the schooner was being loaded to find his wife comforting a distraught Bella.

"You must find my son, Captain Dalton!" she pleaded, grabbing his arm. "Please, you must find him and bring him to me!"

Captain Dalton patted Bella's hand. "I'll do my very best, Miss Bella. Rest assured. I'll radio as soon as I have news."

"Thank you," sobbed Bella. "Thank you."

THE S.S. *Meigle* LEFT ST. JOHN'S LATE THAT SAME evening, filled with goods of all sorts. No one on board could imagine what horrors they were about to see. No one got much sleep that night. Captain Dalton sailed through the night in order to arrive as soon as possible. By late afternoon of the following day he was setting anchor in the harbour. Like the crew of the *Portia*, all hands were agog at the extent of the destruction. How could so much damage have occurred when St. John's was left completely untouched? But there was no time to speculate. Without wasting a minute Captain Dalton and the volunteer doctors and nurses rowed to shore. This time it was not just Mr. Hollett waiting on shore but an entire delegation.

Mr. Hollett reached out and shook Captain Dalton's hand. "Thank you for coming," he said. "I'd like you to meet representatives from all the outports that are in trouble. They've walked or rowed here today so we can coordinate the rescue efforts." Mr. Hollett introduced the men standing on the shore.

Captain Dalton was amazed. "You are so organized!"

"We have to be," said Mr. Hollett shortly. "It is news to you but we are already four days into this disaster. Our people are homeless, hungry and getting sick from shock and exposure. We don't have time to waste." Mr. Hollett had each outport's representative outline what they needed. Captain Dalton began to clench his fists at his sides as the extent of the disaster grew and grew. This was far worse than the Prime Minister – than anybody in St. John's – had imagined. They didn't have nearly enough supplies for everyone. The list went on and on. Forty communities affected, hundreds of homes and outbuildings lost, half of all the boats and fishing equipment of the entire area, most of the winter coal and food, the bulk of the season's catch and no less than twenty-eight lives had been lost, stolen by the sea.

Captain Dalton hardly knew where to begin. "Shall we start unloading the supplies?" The representatives decided on the amount of goods that were to be left with Mr. Hollett for his people. The rest the *Meigle* would deliver as it made its way down the coast, a portion to each community.

"Clearly you need much more than I have," said Captain Dalton. "What is most pressing?"

"Lumber, coal and clothes," replied Mr. Hollett with alacrity. "No question about it. We need lumber to repair and rebuild our homes and coal to keep them warm. It's the middle of November and we've had one blizzard already this week. Our children are walking in the snow in their bare feet. Bronchitis and influenza are spreading."

"Well, we did at least anticipate that," said one of the doctors. "We have lots of medicine." With that he picked up his bag and made his way to the first house he saw. A nurse followed him. Others headed towards the church. Help had finally arrived.

THERE WAS TOO MUCH DEBRIS FOR THE *Meigle* TO leave for the next outport in the dark, so Captain Dalton stayed at anchor overnight. He invited Mr. Hollett on board for dinner. "Tell me more," said the captain. Mr. Hollett drew out the lists that Murphy and Martin had tallied. At the top of his, Martin had scrawled Stuff to Share. Murphy had labelled his list Stolen! There was nothing to smile about in the lists, but the childish writing made both men chuckle.

"These two are born fishermen," smiled Mr. Hollett. "They avoid school as much as humanly possible!"

"That reminds me," said the captain. "Do you know of a boy named Murphy? His mother boards with my wife and she was beside herself when she heard the news. I have promised to send her a message as soon as I know the boy is safe."

"Murphy did this," replied Mr. Hollett, pointing to the Stolen! list. "He's fine. A good lad; in fact, he saved his aunt and cousins from the wave. Without him they'd have surely perished."

"That's excellent news!" sighed the captain. "The first bit of good news today. I was dreading having to send a message to Miss Bella if it was bad news. In the morning I'll collect the boy and bring him on board. His mother wants him home. I hardly blame her."

"Good luck to you on that mission," said Mr. Hollett. "It will probably be easier to supply all the outports with coal than to pry the lad away from here.

Never have I seen one so connected to the sea." Mr. Hollett stood to leave. "But do your duty as you must. Thank you again for your assistance." With a slight bow, Mr. Hollett took his leave and was rowed back to shore.

As soon as the magistrate was gone, Captain Dalton made his way to the radio room. He had the operator prepare a message to Bella. *It will be sent when she arrives at work in the morning,* thought the captain. *She will be so happy to see her son safe and sound when I bring him home.*

"I WON'T GO!" SHOUTED MURPHY. "You need me here!"

"You're an enormous help, Murphy, of course you are," soothed Aunt Rosie. "But right now your mom needs you more. Imagine how she feels, so far away, hearing about the ones what died and not knowing if you be one of them? It makes my heart just about stop even thinking about it."

"It's not forever, son," Uncle Randall said kindly. "There's no fishing for the winter anyway. Go to the city and spend a lovely time with your mom. You'll get to go to a fine school, no doubt, and be able to visit all manner of interesting places."

That was certainly the wrong thing to say. *A fancy school over my dead body,* thought Murphy.

"I'm not running away!" argued Murphy. "Something bad happens to my family, to my home, and I just pick up and leave? I gotta stay, fix it. Make things right. Who's gonna help you build a new house,

Uncle Randall? And I gotta get ready for my mom to come here to live, too." That gave Murphy an idea. "Maybe that's what we should do, Captain Dalton. You go get my mom and bring her here. She's coming anyway as soon as I get a place ready for her. I already told her I was workin' on it. It might take a little longer now, but I can still do it. Can you do that? Go get her and bring her to us?"

Mr. Hollett had not adequately prepared Captain Dalton for Murphy's passionate response. The captain was feeling a little bemused. "I don't think that's a good idea, young man," answered the captain. "The last thing your outport needs right now is more people to look after. Anyway, your mother has a home, a job and a life where she is. And she wants you with her, so that is the end of it." Captain Dalton turned to leave.

"I'll go," said a quiet voice. "Instead of Murphy." The captain whirled around.

"Who are you?"

"I'm Rory, Bella's nephew. I'll go to the city with you."

There was a shocked silence. Murphy was the first to break it. He felt betrayed.

"And you would, wouldn't you? Cut and run? You were plannin' on going anyway and now you've got your excuse! You didn't even tell us. You told everybody else instead. You don't care about us!" Angry tears spilled down Murphy's cheeks. He scrunched his eyes shut. Rory squatted down in front of Murphy and put his hands on the boy's shoulders. Murphy jerked away.

"I love it so much here. How can you hate it?" Murphy whispered.

"I don't hate it, Murph," replied Rory seriously. "I love it too, but in a different way. Do you think I hate our kitchen parties or our chin music or the card games? Do you think my feet could ever forget how to do a jig? Sure, I'd rather be dry than wet and smell like tobacco instead of fish, but that doesn't make me hate the sun that shines down on my face when I'm out in the dory or the sight of an iceberg floating by or the feel of the wind blowing away the clouds. I don't hate my life, Murphy."

"So why do you want to go?" Murphy knuckled the last tear out of his eye. He stared at Rory defiantly. "Why?"

Rory tried earnestly to explain. "Times are changing, Murphy. There's bigger boats out on the water now, bigger than ours, and they're taking more fish than we do. What'll happen if the fish inspector doesn't want our fish, eh? What if he decides to buy his fish from some other fishermen that have lots more than us? What'll we do then?"

Murphy didn't understand. Rory sighed. "I can't make my dad understand either. I'm not running away, Murphy. I'm running *to* someplace else. I have to learn about business, about how we can keep making our living from the sea. I have to learn about those big fish boats, and how they salt all those fish they catch. And when I know how, I'll run right back. I don't want to be a fisherman, Murphy; I want to be a businessman, a businessman in the business of fishing. Do you see?"

Murphy tried to figure out what Rory was trying to say. Finally he shrugged his shoulders. He didn't really understand, but it probably didn't matter to Rory. Murphy turned to his uncle.

"If he goes to the city can I go out in the dory with you?"

Uncle Randall was trying just as hard to understand what his son was telling him. At first he didn't answer Murphy. Then he said, "Hmmmpph. I guess it'll work."

Aunt Rosie started to cry. Murphy thought they were happy tears but he wasn't quite sure. She gave Rory a big hug. "You mind your Aunt Bella, you hear?"

Rory hugged his mom right back. He was so tall now her head could tuck in under his chin. "First thing I'm going to do is help Captain Dalton find all the stuff on Murphy's list. I'll send it to you as soon as I can, okay?" Aunt Rosie's face was still buried in Rory's chest but he could feel her nodding her head. It was decided.

Captain Dalton wasn't sure exactly what had just happened, and he wasn't sure what Miss Bella was going to say when he arrived in St. John's with the wrong boy. No matter, he thought. At least he had somebody to deliver.

CHAPTER 13
Rory's Plans

My dear Murphy,

I was so shocked when I heard of the terrible troubles in the outports! My heart stopped beating, I swear to you. I was so grateful to receive Captain Dalton's message that you were safe. He is a fine man. Rory has told me how you rescued Aunt Rosie and Sean and Fiona. He said something about Annie as well but I must say I didn't quite understand that part of the story.

JUST AS WELL, THOUGHT MURPHY. ANNIE WAS back to being a leaky roof. Every day she had a new idea about building on the headland. Murphy couldn't make her understand that, since his mom wasn't coming, he didn't need a house any more. And now that he was going to be a fisherman, he had more important things on his mind than building play shelters. Annie retorted that it wasn't "playing," it was "planning." Planning for what? He would never understand girls.

I am very proud of you. You behaved with the courage of a grown man. I believe the spirit of your father must have been with you during that terrible night.

Murphy gave a half smile. If his mom only knew how true that was! Deep down, Murphy wasn't sure he'd seen a ghost. What he did know was that his father had been close to his heart that night and that was all that really mattered.

I'm very disappointed that you did not come to the city with Captain Dalton, but I understand your decision. You belong where you are, Murphy, and you are free to stay there. Just as I belong where I am. I love you for wanting to build me a house but just as you cannot come to me, I cannot come to you. We will always be mother and son but will live in different worlds.

Which does not mean to say that we cannot visit. The way your cousin talks, we shall be visiting every month! Rory is a whirlwind of activity. His latest idea is to build a road from the city to the outport! Can you imagine? Motor cars whizzing right across

Newfoundland! Rory thinks it will be easier to deliver supplies to the outports by truck than by schooner, especially in the winter when the harbours freeze. It's hard to imagine such a thing, I tell you.

Mrs. Dalton and I have joined the South Coast Disaster Committee. The government is doing its best to buy supplies and get them delivered to the outports but it is a mammoth task. Everyone in St. John's wants to help. We have organized a door-to-door collection of blankets and clothing. As a matter of fact, one boatload of clothing should have reached you by now.

Yes, it had. Murphy laughed out loud thinking about it. The committee had collected far more girls' clothes than boys' clothes. Albert Rennie had no winter coat and was given a bright red coat with a delicate white lace collar. He was fit to be tied. Given the choice of a red coat or no coat he had to take it. But it was impossible not to tease him every time he went outside.

Everyone wants to help. But still it is difficult to raise enough money to buy the things on your list. Remember I told you about the crash of the stock market? It means that many men are out of work. They have no money to spare. Still, we are trying our best. We have even had donations from England. Tonight Mrs. Dalton is hosting a musical benefit and the Prime Minister is coming. He is the honorary head of the South Coast Disaster Committee.

I must close to get ready for the benefit. Stay well, my son. I love you and hope to see you soon. Preferably NOT by motor car!

All my love, Mother

Murphy smiled. He couldn't imagine riding in a motor car. It would be nice to see his mother more often, though. For so long he had dreamed of living with her in the outport and now the dream was changed. It was a good thing he was too busy really to think about it. The main thing was that he didn't have to go to the city AND he was going to be a real fisherman come spring. That is, if he and Uncle Randall could get enough equipment together. That was the trickiest part. Uncle Randall's paper money had floated out to sea with the family Bible, so they couldn't buy anything. The government said it would help with fishing supplies, but so far no dories, no nets nor handlines had arrived. Uncle Randall said not to worry; it was early days yet. It would be months before the weather allowed them out to fish anyway. Murphy couldn't help but worry. He was finally going to be a fisherman, but what was a fisherman without a boat?

Murphy got out his scribbler. It was easy to get a letter to his mom these days. So many boats were arriving in their harbour delivering building supplies. It was a race against the winter freeze-up.

Dear Mom,

Rory wasn't so busy wen he was here. Guess he's better at being a busnes-man than a fisher-man. Aunt Rosie mises him lots. So does Sean. Fiona misses cabage. She said she wont complain any more now that she's got none. We're ok for carots. They were stil in the ground so the wave never stole them.

We hav a new hous. Its bilt hiher up the hill almost at the meadow so we have to walk longer. But Uncle Randall says its ok we don't hav to worry about no more waves. I helped bild it. My other job is to collect all the pieces from the broken houses and stages. We're tryin to pile up the old wood and put a cover over it to get it dry. We need to burn it cos theres not enuf coal. We wear our coats to bed to kep warm. Its ok but Albert has a red coat and he hates it.

Ember cam back. Ember ran away after the wave and we thot he was ded. But hes back. Sean is hapy. Lots of people went away too. They didn't want to stay after the wave. Its real quiet. There's no parties. We need a party with music like you have. Maybe I shud make a ugly stik.

Happy Christmas from your son Murphy

CHAPTER 14
Are Mummers Allowed In?
December 26, 1929

MURPHY COULDN'T BELIEVE IT. HE HELD the glorious ball in his hand and examined it from all sides. An orange! Even in good times an orange at Christmas was hard to come by, but this year it seemed like a miracle. A schooner had arrived from the southern United States with oranges for everybody. The sailors said the folks down there felt bad about the tidal wave. Well, it was a pretty wonderful gift. Nails and window glass and coal were probably more useful but far less tasty.

Murphy tucked his orange under his pillow. He decided to save it. All in all, it was not the best Christmas ever. Most everybody had a roof over their heads and that was good. But now that the first big problem was taken care of the whole outport filled up with worry. What next? The government had promised boats and fishing gear for the spring, but there wasn't enough money left in the disaster fund to cover a winter's worth of food or coal. And there were months left of winter.

Murphy wandered out to the kitchen. There wasn't much to do. Aunt Rosie's knitting needles were flying away, just like usual. Lots of the ladies in St. John's had extra wool, so great crates of yarn had been donated. All the outport moms were knitting all day and practically all night to replace the long underwear, the jerseys, the hats and mitts and sweaters that had gone out to sea. Sometimes Murphy thought of that old talking codfish from Mr. Inkpen's story. Maybe all his seventeen children were wearing sweaters now, down at the bottom of the sea. Murphy smiled. He wouldn't mind that special tablecloth right about now. "Spread, cloth, spread!" And there would be lassie buns and brewis and scrunchins and tea with molasses. Now that would be lovely.

Uncle Randall was whittling. Most winters he'd be working on fixing the holes in his nets but this winter, well, no nets. There was lots of wood though. So night after night Uncle Randall carved miniature dories and tiny fish. They weren't very good but it kept Uncle Randall's hands busy. Murphy plunked himself down on the daybed. Sean and Fiona were reading. Nix on that, thought Murphy. Too much like school. He wished they still had a radio. Maybe he should start working on an ugly stick, like he'd told his mom. It would be something to do.

Just then, there was a loud pounding on the door. Aunt Rosie started. "Who'd be bothering to knock at this hour?" she spluttered. They all five looked at the door.

It creaked open. Four masked creatures pushed in.

"Any mummers allowed in?"

Aunt Rosie's face split into a grin. Murphy hadn't seen her do that since the wave. Fiona jumped up on the daybed and clapped her hands. Uncle Randall put down his whittling knife and leaned back in the rocker. Sean raced over to the mummers and started to poke them.

"I'm a good guesser! I'll figure out who they are!" shouted Sean. He poked the mummers some more. "I don't know them," said Sean curiously.

There was lots of scope for poking. One of the mummers was wearing a long flannelette nightgown overtop a pair of fisherman's oilskins. Pillows had been stuffed into the oilskins making the mummer as fat as Santa Claus. That one has to be a man, thought Murphy, judging from the size of the gumboots on his feet. He was wearing a paper crown on his head. Attached to the crown was an old lace curtain that completely covered the mummer's face.

The second mummer was shorter. This one had about four big plaid shirts on, one over the other. The shirttails hung to the mummer's knees. Small gumboots this time, pulled over thick winter longjohns.

The longjohns had a trap door in the back and the mummer was wearing them back to front. The trap door was stuffed with a pillow, making the belly as big as the first mummer's. A straw hat adorned with feathers disguised the face. It was attached to a veil that completed covered the mummer's head.

The third mummer was wearing a wedding gown. This one had a pillowcase over its head with little eye-holes cut out and kissy lips drawn on with lipstick. The last one was so tall he nearly touched the ceiling. He'd built himself a pair of bosoms that stuck out about three feet!

Sean jumped up and grabbed one of the bosoms. "Not real!" he shouted with glee. "This one's a man!"

Fiona got into the game. "Are you from here?" Two mummers nodded yes. The other two shook their heads. It was a mystery, for sure.

"Are you Hilliers?"

Raspy, disguised voices croaked, "No!"

"Are you Rennies?"

"No!"

"Do you fish?"

"No!"

"Do you dance?"

That was their cue. The small one with the plaid shirts pulled a fiddle from a sack and started a tune. The tall one adjusted his bosoms then leapt into a jig. His big gumboots stomped out a rhythm that got faster and faster. The tall mummer grabbed Aunt

Rosie's hands and pulled her into the dance. The mummer wearing the wedding dress delicately offered her hand to Uncle Randall and they joined in too. Murphy and Fiona clapped while Sean continued his poking. All of a sudden he put his hands over his mouth and let out a great peal of laughter.

"It's Rory, it's Rory!" he shouted. Everybody looked at the tall mummer in astonishment. "Look at the way he dances!"

Rory pulled off his mask with a flourish. Then he executed a neat little jig for good measure. "It is I," he said with a bow, "your prodigal son!"

Fiona threw herself into her brother's arms. Sean was rolling on the floor with laughter. Tears were streaming down Aunt Rosie's face. What a time! But Murphy was still pondering. If that was Rory, who were the others?

Murphy stared and stared at the mummer with the fiddle. "Are you from St. John's?" he asked. The mummer nodded.

"Did you come on a boat?" This time all three masked mummers nodded.

"Did you get here today?" More nods.

Murphy was clearly on to something. The rest of the family looked at him expectantly. Could he guess? Murphy looked over at Rory. Rory was grinning all over his face. Could it be?

"Mom?" asked Murphy hesitantly. "Is it you?"

Bella tore off the feathered hat and held out her

arms. Murphy rushed into them. "Mom!" he cried joyously. There were shrieks and cheers and tears all around. In the confusion, Sean snuck up to the remaining mummers and pulled off their masks. It was Captain Randall and a lady. "Are you Mrs. Captain?" asked Sean. Cora Dalton smiled and nodded her head. The captain and his wife appeared a little bewildered by all the activity. It was long minutes before Aunt Rosie remembered herself and got them a cup of tea.

Just then Annie stuck her head in at the door. "What's all the noise?" she asked. Then she caught sight of the mummers and hightailed it back to her own house shouting at the top of her lungs.

"They got mummers! Come on and look! They got mummers!"

In no time at all it seemed every single person in the outport was crowded into Aunt Rosie's kitchen. Everybody was talking at once. It was a madhouse, so finally Uncle Randall shouted them all down. "Let the mummers talk, will ya?"

Bella started their story. "I wanted so badly to see Murphy," she began, squeezing her son's hand. "Rory was doing a wonderful job getting donations to send to you all…"

"Hear, hear!" murmured the crowd. Rory smiled at his friends and neighbours.

"…and Captain Dalton looked at the weather report and thought he could make one more trip before the harbour froze. Mrs. Dalton and I thought we might as well come along for the ride!" Bella gave Murphy another hug.

"And what better way to surprise you all than to come as Christmas mummers!"

Everyone in the kitchen cheered. Old Mrs. Inkpen had tears rolling down her cheeks. "I didn't think we'd have any mummering this year," she wept. "Too many trials to have fun. But here they are!"

Captain Dalton had been quiet up till then. "Please, can somebody explain about mummering? Bella told us what to wear and how to act, but Cora and I are unfamiliar with the tradition."

Mr. Inkpen cleared his throat. "We're hard-working folk here in the outports," he began. "All year the men work; all year the women work. We don't lie; we don't steal; we look after one another. We're good right up to Christmas. Then watch out! That's when we stop being who we are. Men dress as women; women dress as men. We play tricks, beg for cake, even have a drop of whiskey! We dance and we sing and, as long as our disguises are good, no one knows who we are. For twelve days after Christmas right is left and up is down. Then we take the mummer's key and lock Christmas away for another year. The disguises are put away and we're grateful for who we really are. That's mummering."

There were nods of agreement throughout the room. Mr. Inkpen had a fine way of saying things.

"You mummers, don't tell me you forgot the key to Christmas?" demanded Mr. Inkpen.

"We did not," replied Rory. From his pocket he drew out a massive key. It was cut from cardboard and painted silver. Somebody had glued sparkles all over it.

"Wow," breathed Annie. "I've never seen such a fancy mummer's key!"

"Nobody has," said Rory. "This is a special one. Aunt Bella thought it up. This key is not only going to lock up Christmas, it's going to lock up all our troubles." Rory stuck the key into Sean's belly and pretended to turn it, making him giggle.

"Lock up Christmas!" he shouted.

He stuck the key in Fiona's belly. "Lock up the big wave!"

He stuck the key in Albert's belly. "Lock up the tears!"

Sean grabbed the key and poked it into Rory's belly. "Lock up my brother!"

Fiona grabbed it next. "Lock up the cabbages!"

Amidst all the laughter, Bella took Murphy's hand and drew him outside. "I have a present for you," she said. "Look."

Stacked up neatly beside the house was a large pile of wood. There were big beams, the kind used to construct the frame of a drying flake. And there were lots of smaller pieces too. Murphy's eyes sparkled.

"A person could build a fine flake with all that wood!" he said in excitement.

"A person certainly could," smiled his mother. "And a man like yourself definitely could."

Murphy gave his mother a tight hug. "How'd you know that's what I wanted most?"

"It was easy," she said. "It was right on your list." Bella reached into the trap door of the oversized longjohns she was still wearing. She drew out a crumpled piece of paper and carefully unrolled it. Across the top was written in bold, rather crooked letters, "Stolen!" And down at the very bottom was written: Murphy and Annie: one stage, one flake.

"That's my list!" gasped Murphy in surprise. "But I didn't write that on it! How'd you get it?"

"The Prime Minister himself gave it to me when he was finished reading it," replied Bella. "I kept it with me every day. It proved that you were still alive, not stolen by the wave." Bella gave Murphy another hug. "I love you, Son."

Murphy smiled. "I love you too, Mom. How long can you stay?"

"Just a few days. We're racing the ice."

"Well then," said Murphy. "You'd better get that fiddle back out, don't ya think? We got a lot of dancing to do!"

Music and laughter spilled through the doorway. The two of them went back inside. Murphy searched out Rory.

"Rory, I gave the Prime Minister's list to you," he asked suspiciously. "How'd 'Murphy and Annie's stage' get on the list?"

"Dunno," said Rory with a smile.

"It looks like your handwriting," Murphy persisted. "Rory, how'd you know?"

"How do you think you got all the lumber to build it in the first place?" asked Rory. "Did you think it just appeared out of thin air?"

Murphy was astounded. "It was you?" he asked in wonder.

Rory looked straight into Murphy's eyes. "It wasn't hard to figure out what the pair of you were up to, kid. My father needs someone who loves the sea, someone who will fight it by his side day after day. That someone isn't me, Murph; it's you. It was the only way I knew to help."

Murphy was speechless. Rory clapped him on the shoulder and turned to go back to the dancing. Murphy had one last thought, and called out after him.

"Rory, thanks for the light that night I was looking for Annie. It really helped."

Rory looked back quizzically. "What light?" he asked.

Murphy didn't answer. A slow smile spread across his face. His heart felt warm. He looked around at all the people he loved and couldn't help himself. His feet started to dance.

AUTHOR'S NOTE

A Terrible Roar of Water IS CALLED HISTORICAL fiction. That means that some things in the book really happened and others did not. But which is which?

THE TSUNAMI

In spite of the fact that tsunamis are very rare in the Atlantic Ocean, on November 18, 1929 at 7:30 p.m. one really did hit the coast of Newfoundland. It was caused by an undersea earthquake. The earthquake registered 7.2 on the Richter scale and the shaking was felt as far east as Montreal and as far south as New York City. The earthquake caused the ocean floor to crack and the seabed to slip, creating three huge waves. The waves hit the coast of Newfoundland at speeds of up to sixty miles per hour, affecting 13,000 people living in seventy-eight communities. Fifty of those outports were devastated by the disaster.

Some people call tsunamis "tidal waves" but that isn't really correct. Tsunamis are related to earthquakes, and tidal waves are the result of the gravitational forces of the moon. Tsunamis get their name from two Japanese words: *tsu* meaning harbour and *nami* meaning wave. It's only fair that Japan gets to choose the name for these terrible waves, as they suffer more tsunamis than any other country in the world. Eighty percent of all tsunamis occur in the Pacific Ocean.

Some people say that animals can tell if a tsunami is coming, but it has never been proven. Newspaper reporters in Sri Lanka noticed that elephants started to head inland just before a tsunami hit the coast in 2004. Strangely, when the people of that area realized that something was wrong, they headed *towards* the water instead of *away* from it. Many of them drowned as a result.

Check out the link below for a really cool animation of the wave paths from the tsunami in the Indian Ocean in 2004. It's cool from a scientific point of view, even though it's hard to forget that that tsunami was one of the deadliest natural disasters in recorded history. The hundred-foot waves killed 225,000 people in eleven countries. Indonesia, Sri Lanka, India and Thailand were the hardest hit.

http://nctr.pmel.noaa.gov/animations/Sumatra2004-cmoore.mov

THE PEOPLE

All of the *Disaster Strikes!* books have both real and imaginary characters. The question is – which are which? Before you read on, think for a moment about whether or not Murphy is real.

What did you decide? If you thought he was imaginary, you were right. In fact, Murphy's whole family came out of my head. So did Annie. But many of the people in the book and the things they did or said are part of real life history. To find out about the real people, I consulted the historical records and lots of books and read the first-person accounts told by those who survived the tsunami. And here's what I learned from them:

Nurse Cherry was very real. Her actions immediately after the disaster helped to save many lives. In fact, she worked so hard and for so long that the Chairman of the Board of Health who arrived on the S.S. *Meigle* practically had to kidnap her to make sure she had a rest before she collapsed.

The Rennie family was real, too. Their house did float out to sea and back again and, sadly, Mrs. Rennie and several of her children were lost to the waves. Except, of course, Margaret. She really was saved by sinking the house in The Pond. The Hilliers, the Kellys and the Hipditchs were real, as were the Brushetts and the Walsh sisters. Everything that happens to them in this book is part of the historical record.

The real Mrs. Moulton did raise sheep. She thought the earthquake was the doing of ghosts.

Mr. and Mrs. Inkpen were also real and rescued by the neighbours when their flake broke apart. But I made up the part about Mr. Inkpen being a storyteller. He was well respected in the community…so it *could* have been true!

STORYTELLING

Once upon a time when wishing still helped…

In Newfoundland, telling stories is a very popular pastime and good storytellers are favoured visitors. The question is: are the stories Murphy hears at the kitchen party real…or not?

"Jack" tales are commonplace in many parts of the world. Jack is sometimes the clever one, sometimes the silly one and sometimes the tricky one. But he almost always wins the day. I made up the story from several different Jack tales all put together.

The story of the sealer's ghost is reputed to be true. It happened to a boy and his father who came from an outport north of St. John's around 1875. Lots of people tell this story in many different ways. In some versions of the story, the father speaks to his son using the voice of a seal pup. The story of the magic writing appeared around 1837. It was told to a sea captain by a man named Bruce who said that it was true. After all these years, who are we to say? Stories about people who can magically see the future are told all over the world.

Storytelling is an "up-close-and-personal" form of communication. When the battery-operated radio became available, it began to replace storytelling. Then electricity came, and finally television. In the rest of Canada, the stories that came out of these story boxes made storytelling practically disappear. But in Newfoundland, storytelling has remained popular. Outport people listen to the radio and watch television just like everybody else, but they have never forgotten the joy that comes from a story told heart to heart.

PARTY TIME!

One of the things I enjoyed writing about most in this book was the outport itself. I loved the idea that everybody knew everybody else (including their business!) and that it was okay to march into somebody's kitchen and plunk down on the daybed for a chat. I loved the music and the dancing and the jokes and, most of all, the caring for one another. Sometimes I wished I'd lived in an outport too.

Newfoundland has a rich artistic heritage that continues today. In part it may have developed because the area was so isolated. It may have developed because the winters were long and hard and the people had to make their own entertainment. Whatever the reason, the artists of Newfoundland have contributed a great deal to the traditions of Canada.

As well as studying jokes (that was a fun project!) I liked studying the customs of the outport people, like the gumboots in the kitchen and the hoops used when carrying buckets. Here are a few of the things I learned that didn't make it into the book:

- If a child has asthma, cut off a lock of her or his hair, drill a hole in a tree, and hide the hair inside it. It will make the asthma go away – eventually.
- For a sore throat, tie a salt herring around your neck.
- For a cough, take the bark off a white spruce tree. Scrape the inside of the bark into a pot and boil it. Add some molasses to soothe the cough.
- For a bad chest, save the grease from the Christmas goose and rub it on the chest and back.
- Don't use seal fat to make soap. It has a horrible smell.
- Use old flour sacks dyed black to make kids' trousers. When you knit socks, don't leave them white; they get too dirty. Dye socks brown by boiling the moss off the spruce tree.

Imagine not being able to call a doctor or a dentist or go to a store to pick up groceries or clothes.

The outport people had to know a great many things to survive.

I particularly enjoyed learning about the kitchen parties. If you want to see real mummers in action or listen to the sound of an ugly stick, there are some interesting videos on YouTube. Type in "Lois and the Ugly Stick" or "The Mummer's Song by Simani" and just try to keep your toes from tapping!

THE SALT COD FISHERY

When John Cabot discovered Newfoundland in 1497, he also found the Grand Banks. The Grand Banks is a group of shallow underwater shelves just off the coast of Newfoundland. Cool water coming from the north collides with warm water coming from the south and the result is lots of food for fish. So huge schools of fish like cod, haddock and capelin live on the Grand Banks, and that makes for some of the best fishing in the world. As soon as Cabot took this news back to Europe, many countries like France, Portugal and Spain rushed to stake a claim on the rich fishing grounds.

The British were particularly interested in the area. But there was a problem. Fish caught in Newfoundland might not make it to market in Europe for months. There were no refrigerators. In order to make sure the fish didn't spoil before arriving home, sailors used salt to preserve the catch.

But the British didn't have a lot of salt. So they developed a technique that used the sun and the wind to help dry the catch, which meant less salt was needed. The only catch was that it took time and space, so "light-salt" fishermen needed to take their catch to land quickly and do the preserving there. So the British decided to set up fishing villages in Newfoundland, places where they could preserve the fish before loading it on big boats destined for Britain. These villages were called "outports," which was a British word used for any British port located outside of London.

It turned out that the "light-salt" technique made for a much tastier fish. Soon the outport fish were prized throughout the world, bringing a much higher price than regular salt cod.

The undersea earthquake that caused the tsunami may be partly responsible for the fact that fewer fish live on the Grand Banks today. What is for sure is that after 1929 fish stocks began to disappear. Another reason for this may be the big fish boats that Rory was worried about. The big boats took too many fish at one time. The result is that today few people can make their living as fishermen, and those that do must work very hard. So the last question is this: will the outports survive?

For more on the salt cod fishery and some great photos and videos of fish guts(!), check out: *http://www.therooms.ca/ic_sites/fisheries/student.asp?frame=off.*

ACKNOWLEDGEMENTS

MANY THANKS TO THE CANADIAN CENTRE FOR FOLK Culture Studies and to the Folklore Department of Memorial University for research materials, and most particularly to the tsunami survivors who have told their stories. I would also like to thank the many writers and researchers who have compiled information about this particular place and time, such as Maura Hanrahan, Garry Cranford, Claire Mowat, Rosemary Ommer, Hilda Chaulk Murray and Margaret Robertson.

My ongoing appreciation goes to the members of the Victoria Storytellers' Guild. Even though these days I hide away with my computer, my "story box," I know you're there and take vicarious pleasure in all that you do.

To Laura, thanks for making it all work. And Barbara, your comments are always integral to the work and highly valued.

And last, but never least, to Dale.

ABOUT THE AUTHOR

PENNY DRAPER IS AN AUTHOR, a bookseller and a storyteller who lives in Victoria, BC. Originally from Toronto, she received a degree in Literature from Trinity College, University of Toronto and attended the Storytellers' School of Toronto. For many years, Penny shared tales as a professional storyteller at schools, libraries, conferences, festivals and on radio and television. She has told stories in an Arabian harem and from inside a bear's belly – but that is a story in itself.

Penny Draper's first juvenile fiction novel, *Terror at Turtle Mountain*, was a finalist for the Silver Birch Young Reader's Choice Award in Ontario, as well as the Diamond Willow Award, the Geoffrey Bilson Award for Historical Fiction for Young People and Book of the Year for the ForeWord Magazine Awards in the US. It is part of Coteau Books for Kids *Disaster Strikes!* series. The series also includes Penny's second book, *Peril at Pier Nine*, and *The Graveyard of the Sea*.

Coteau Books has chosen to print this book on Rolland Enviro100 instead of virgin fibres. By doing so we have reduced our ecological footprint by :

Tree(s): 17
Solid waste : 498 kg
Water : 47 137 L
Air emissions : 1 094 kg

0617-7976